Dear Reader,

I really can't express how flattered I am and also how grateful I am to Harlequin Books for releasing this collection of my published works. It came as a great surprise. I never think of myself as writing books that are collectible. In fact, there are days when I forget that writing is work at all. What I do for a living is so much fun that it never seems like a job. And since I reside in a small community, and my daily life is confined to such mundane things as feeding the wild birds and looking after my herb patch in the backyard, I feel rather unconnected from what many would think of as a glamorous profession.

But when I read my email, or when I get letters from readers, or when I go on signing trips to bookstores to meet all of you, I feel truly blessed. Over the past thirty years I have made lasting friendships with many of you. And quite frankly, most of you are like part of my family. You can't imagine how much you enrich my life. Thank you so much.

I also need to extend thanks to my family (my husband, James, son, Blayne, daughter-in-law, Christina, and granddaughter, Selena Marie), to my best friend, Ann, to my readers, booksellers and the wonderful people at Harlequin Books—from my editor of many years, Tara, to all the other fine and talented people who make up our publishing house. Thanks to all of you for making this job and my private life so worth living.

Thank you for this tribute, Harlequin, and for putting up with me for thirty long years! Love to all of you.

Diana Palmer

P9-DYE-842

DIANA PALMER

The prolific author of more than a hundred books, Diana Palmer got her start as a newspaper reporter. A multi–*New York Times* bestselling author and one of the top ten romance writers in America, she has a gift for telling the most sensual tales with charm and humor. Diana lives with her family in Cornelia, Georgia.

Visit her website at www.DianaPalmer.com.

THE Essential COLLECTION

New York Times and *USA TODAY* Bestselling Author

DIANA PALMER

ETHAN

TORONTO NEW YORK LONDON
AMSTERDAM PARIS SYDNEY HAMBURG
STOCKHOLM ATHENS TOKYO MILAN MADRID
PRAGUE WARSAW BUDAPEST AUCKLAND

Recycling programs
for this product may
not exist in your area.

ISBN-13: 978-0-373-36366-7

ETHAN

Copyright © 1990 by Diana Palmer

Printed in U.S.A.

New York Times and *USA TODAY*
Bestselling Author

Diana Palmer

The Essential Collection
Long, Tall Texans...and More!

Chapter One

Arabella was drifting. She seemed to be floating along on a particularly fast cloud, high above the world. She murmured contentedly and sank into the fluffy nothingness, aware somewhere of a fleeting pain that began to grow with every passing second until it was a white-hot throb in one of her hands.

"No!" she exclaimed, and her eyes flew open.

She was lying on a cold table. Her dress, her beautiful gray dress, was covered with blood and she felt bruised and cut all over. A man in a white jacket was examining her eyes. She groaned.

"Concussion," the man murmured. "Abrasions, contusions. Compound fracture of the wrist, one ligament almost severed. Type and cross-match her blood, prep her for surgery, and get me an operating room."

"Yes, Doctor."

"Well?" The other voice was harsh, demanding. Very male and familiar, but not her father's.

"She'll be all right," the doctor said with resignation. "Now, will you please go outside and sit down, Mr. Hardeman? While I can appreciate your concern—" and that was an understatement, the physician thought "—you can do her more good by letting us work."

Ethan! The voice was Ethan's! She managed to turn her head, and yes, it was Ethan Hardeman. He looked as if they'd dragged him out of bed. His black hair was rumpled, apparently by his own fingers. His hard, lean face was drawn, his gray eyes so dark with worry that they looked black. His white shirt was half-unbuttoned, as if he'd thrown it on, and his dark jacket was open. He'd all but crushed the brim of the creamy Stetson in his hand.

"Bella," he breathed when he saw her pale, damaged face.

"Ethan," she managed in a hoarse whisper. "Oh, Ethan, my hand!"

His expression tautened as he moved closer to her, despite the doctor's protests. He reached down and touched her poor, bruised cheek. "Baby, what a scare you gave me!" he whispered. His hand actually seemed to be trembling as he brushed back her disheveled long brown hair. Her green eyes were bright with pain and welcome, all mixed up together.

"My father?" she asked with apprehension, because he'd been driving the car.

"They flew him to Dallas. He had an ocular injury, and they've got some of the top men in the field there.

He's all right, otherwise. He couldn't take care of you, so he had the hospital call me." Ethan smiled coldly. "God knows, that was a gut-wrenching decision on his part."

She was in too much pain to pick up on the meaning behind the words. "But…my hand?" she asked.

He stood up straight. "They'll talk to you about that later. Mary and the rest will be here in the morning. I'll stay until you're out of surgery."

She caught at his arm with her good hand, feeling the hard muscle tighten. "Make them understand…how important my hand is, please," she pleaded.

"They understand. They'll do what can be done." He touched her cracked lips gently with his forefinger. "I won't leave you," he said quietly. "I'll be here."

She grabbed his hand, holding it, feeling his strength, drawing on his strength for the first time in recent memory. "Ethan," she whispered as the pain built, "remember the swimming hole…?"

His expression closed up. He actually flinched as her face contorted. "My God, can't you give her something?" he asked the doctor, as if the pain were his own.

The doctor seemed to understand at last that it was more than bad temper driving the tall, angry man who'd stormed into the emergency room barely ten minutes ago. The look on those hard features as he'd held the woman's hand had said everything.

"I'll give her something," the doctor promised. "Are you a relative? Her husband, perhaps?"

Ethan's silver eyes cut at him. "No, I'm not a relative. She's a concert pianist, very commercial these days.

She lives with her father and she's never been allowed to marry."

The doctor didn't have time for discussion. He settled Ethan with a nurse and vanished gratefully into the emergency room.

Hours later, Arabella drifted in and out of the anesthesia in a private room. Ethan was there again, staring angrily out the window at the pastel colors of the sky at dawn, still in the same clothes he'd been wearing the night before. Arabella was in a floral hospital gown and she felt as she probably looked—weak and wrung out.

"Ethan," she called.

He turned immediately, going to the bedside. He did look terrible, all right. His face was white with strain and bridled anger.

"How are you?" he asked.

"Tired and sore and groggy," she murmured, trying to smile at him. He looked so fierce, just as he had when they were younger. She was almost twenty-three now, and Ethan was thirty, but he'd always been worlds ahead of her in maturity. With Ethan standing over her, it was hard to remember the anguish of the past four years. So many memories, she thought drowsily, watching that dear face. Ethan had been her heart four years ago, but he'd married Miriam. Ethan had forced Miriam into a separation only a little while after they married, but she'd fought Ethan's divorce action tooth and nail for almost four years. Miriam had given up, at last, this year. Their divorce had only become final three months ago.

Ethan was a past master at hiding his feelings, but

the deep lines in his face spoke for themselves. Miriam had hurt him dreadfully. Arabella had tried to warn him, in her own shy way. They'd argued over Miriam and because of it, Ethan had shut Arabella out of his life with cold cruelty. She'd seen him in passing since then because she and his sister-in-law were best friends, and visits were inevitable. But Ethan had been remote and unapproachable. Until last night.

"You should have listened to me about Miriam," she said groggily.

"We won't talk about my ex-wife," he said coldly. "You're coming home with me when you're able to get around again. Mother and Mary will look after you and keep you company."

"How's my father?" she asked.

"I haven't found out anything new. I'll check later. Right now, I need breakfast and a change of clothes. I'll come back as soon as I've got my men started at home. We're in the middle of roundup."

"What a time to be landed with me," she said with a deep sigh. "I'm sorry, Ethan. Dad could have spared you this."

He ignored the comment. "Did you have any clothes in the car with you?"

She shook her head. The slight movement hurt, so she stopped. She reached up with her free hand to smooth back the mass of waving dark brown hair from her bruised face. "My clothes are back in the apartment in Houston."

"Where's the key?"

"In my purse. They should have brought it in with me," she murmured drowsily.

He searched in the locker on the other side of the

room and found her expensive leather purse. He carried it to the bed with the air of a man holding a poisonous snake. "Where is it?" he muttered.

She stared at him, amused despite the sedatives and the growing pain. "The key is in the zipper compartment," she managed.

He took out a set of keys and she showed him the right one. He put the purse away with obvious relief. "Beats me why women can't use pockets, the way men do."

"The stuff we carry wouldn't fit into pockets," she said reasonably. She laid back on the pillows, her eyes open and curious. "You look terrible."

He didn't smile. He hardly ever had, except for a few magical days when she was eighteen. Before Miriam got her beautiful hands on him. "I haven't had much sleep," he said, his voice sharp and cutting.

She smiled drowsily. "Don't growl at me. Coreen wrote to me last month in Los Angeles. She said you're impossible to live with these days."

"My mother always thought I was impossible to live with," he reminded her.

"She said you'd been that way for three months, since the divorce was final," she replied. "Why did Miriam finally give in? She was the one who insisted on staying married to you, despite the fact that she stopped living with you ages ago."

"How should I know?" he asked abruptly, and turned away.

She saw the way he closed up at the mention of his ex-wife's name, and her heart felt heavy and cold. His marriage had hurt her more than anything in her life. It had been unexpected, and she'd almost gone off the deep end when she'd heard. Somehow she'd always thought that Ethan cared for her. She'd been too young for him at eighteen, but that day by the swimming hole, she'd been sure that he felt more than just a physical attraction for her. Or maybe that had been one more hopeless illusion. Whatever he'd felt, he'd started going around with Miriam immediately after that sweet interlude, and within two months he'd married the woman.

Arabella had mourned him bitterly. He'd been the first man in her life in all the important ways, except for the most intimate one. She was still waiting for that first intimacy, just as she'd waited most of her adult life for Ethan to love her. She almost laughed out loud. Ethan had never loved her. He'd loved Miriam, who'd come to the ranch to film a commercial. She'd watched it happen, watched Ethan falling under the spell of the green-eyed, redheaded model with her sophisticated beauty.

Arabella had never had the measure of self-confidence and teasing sophistication that Miriam had. And Miriam had walked off with Ethan, only to leave him. They said that Ethan had become a woman-hater because of his marriage. Arabella didn't doubt it. He'd never been a playboy in the first place. He was much too serious and stoical. There was nothing happy-go-lucky or carefree about Ethan. He'd had the responsibility for his family for a long time now, and even Arabella's earliest memories of him were of a quiet, hard man who threw out orders like a commanding general, intimidating men twice his age when he was only just out of his teens.

Ethan was watching her, but his scrutiny ceased

when she noticed him standing beside the bed. "I'll send someone to your apartment in Houston for your things."

"Thank you." He wouldn't talk to her about Miriam. Somehow, she'd expected that reaction. She took a deep breath and started to lift her hand. It felt heavy. She looked down and realized that it was in a small cast. Red antiseptic peeked out from under it, stark against her pale skin. She felt the threat of reality and withdrew from it, closing her eyes.

"They had to set the bones," Ethan said. "The cast comes off in six weeks, and you'll have the use of your hand again."

Use of it, yes. But would she be able to play again as she had? How long would it take, and how would she manage to support herself and her father if she couldn't? She felt panic seeping in. Her father had a heart condition. She knew, because he'd used it against her in the early days when she hadn't wanted the years of study, the eternal practice that made it impossible for her to go places with her friends Mary and Jan, Ethan's sister, and Matt, his brother whom Mary had later married.

It was astonishing that her father had called Ethan after the wreck. Ever since Arabella had blossomed into a young woman, her father had made sure that Ethan didn't get too close to her. He'd never liked Ethan. The reverse was also true. Arabella hadn't understood the friction, because Ethan had never made any serious advances toward her, until that day she and Ethan had gone swimming at the creek, and things had almost gone too far. Arabella had told no one, so her father hadn't known about that. It was her own private, special secret. Hers and Ethan's.

She forced her mind back to the present. She couldn't let herself become maudlin now. She had enough complications in her life without asking for more. She vaguely remembered mentioning to Ethan that day she and he had gone swimming together, when she was eighteen. She hoped against hope that he'd been too worried to pay attention to the remark, that she hadn't given away how precious the memory was to her.

"You said I'd stay with you," she began falteringly, trying to make her mind work. "But, my father...?"

"Your uncle lives in Dallas, remember?" he asked curtly. "Your father will probably stay there."

"He won't like having me this far away," she said doggedly.

"No, he won't, will he?" He pulled the sheet up to her chin. "Try to sleep. Let the medicine work."

Her wide green eyes opened, holding his. "You don't want me at your house," she said huskily. "You never did. We quarreled over Miriam and you said I was a pain in the neck and you never wanted to have to see me again!"

He actually winced. "Try to sleep," he said tersely.

She was drifting in and out of consciousness, blissfully unaware of the tortured look on the dark face above her. She closed her eyes. "Yes. Sleep..."

The world seemed very far away as the drugs took hold at last and she slept. Her dreams were full of the old days, of growing up with Mary and Matt, of Ethan always nearby, beloved and taciturn and completely unattainable. No matter how hard she tried to act her age, Ethan had never looked at her as a woman in those early days.

Arabella had always loved him. Her music had been her escape. She could play the exquisite classical pieces and put all the love Ethan didn't want into her fingers as she played. It was that fever and need that had given her a start in the musical world. At the age of twenty-one, she'd won an international competition with a huge financial prize, and the recognition had given her a shot at a recording contract.

Classical music was notoriously low-paying for pianists, but Arabella's style had caught on quickly when she tried some pop pieces. The albums had sold well, and she was asked to do more. The royalties began to grow, along with her fame.

Her father had pushed her into personal appearances and tours, and, basically shy in front of people she didn't know, she'd hated the whole idea of it. She'd tried to protest, but her father had dominated her all her life, and she hadn't had the will to fight him. Incredible, that, she told herself, when she could stand up to Ethan and most other people without a qualm. Her father was different. She loved him and he'd been her mainstay when her mother had died so long ago. She couldn't bear to hurt her father by refusing his guidance in her career. Ethan had hated the hold her father had on her, but he'd never asked her to try to break it.

Over the years, while she was growing up in Jacobsville, Ethan had been a kind of protective but distant big brother. Until that day he'd taken her swimming down at the creek and everything had changed. Miriam had been at the ranch even then, starting on a layout with a Western theme for a fashion magazine. Ethan had paid her very little notice until he'd almost lost control with Arabella when they started kissing, but after that day he'd begun pursuing Miriam. It hadn't taken long.

Arabella had heard Miriam bragging to another model that she had the Hardeman fortune in the palm of her hand and that she was going to trade Ethan her body for a life of luxury. It had sickened Arabella to think of the man she loved being treated as a meal ticket and nothing more, so she'd gone to him and tried to tell him what she'd heard.

He hadn't believed her. He'd accused her of being jealous of Miriam. He'd hurt her with his cold remarks about her age and inexperience and naïveté, then he'd ordered her off the ranch. She'd run away, all the way out of the state and back to music school.

How strange that Ethan should be the one to look after her. It was the first time she'd ever been in a hospital, the first time she'd been anything except healthy. She wouldn't have expected Ethan to bother with her, despite her father's request. Ethan had studiously ignored Arabella since his marriage, right down to deliberately disappearing every time she came to visit Mary and Coreen.

Mary and Matt lived with Matt and Ethan's mother, Coreen, at the big rambling Hardeman house. Coreen always welcomed Arabella as if she were family when she came to spend an occasional afternoon with her friend Mary. But Ethan was cold and unapproachable and barely spoke to her.

Arabella hadn't expected more from Ethan, though. He'd made his opinion of her crystal clear when he'd announced his engagement to Miriam shortly after he'd started dating the model. The engagement had shocked everyone, even his mother, and the rushed wedding had been a source of gossip for months. But Miriam wasn't pregnant, so obviously he'd married her for love. If that was the case, it was a brief love. Miriam had gone, bag and baggage, six months later, leaving Ethan alone but not unattached. Arabella had never learned why Miriam had refused the divorce or why Miriam had started running around on a man she'd only just married. It was one of many things about his marriage that Ethan never discussed with anyone.

Arabella felt oblivion stealing her away. She gave in to it at last, sighing as she fell asleep, leaving all her worries and heartaches behind.

Chapter Two

When Arabella woke up again, it was daylight. Her hand throbbed in its white cast. She ground her teeth together, recalling the accident all too vividly—the impact, the sound of broken glass, her own cry, and then oblivion rushing over her. She couldn't blame the accident on her father; it had been unavoidable. Slick roads, a car that pulled out in front of them, and they'd gone off the pavement and into a telephone pole. She was relieved to be alive, despite the damage to her hand. But she was afraid her father wasn't going to react well to the knowledge that her performing days might be over. She refused to think about that possibility. She had to be optimistic.

Belatedly she wondered what had become of the car they'd been driving. They'd been on their way to Jacobsville from Corpus Christi, where she'd been

performing in a charity concert. Her father hadn't told
her why they were going to Jacobsville, so she'd assumed
that they were taking a brief vacation in their old home
town. She'd thought then about seeing Ethan again,
and her heart had bounced in her chest. But she hadn't
expected to see him under these circumstances.

They'd been very close to Jacobsville, so naturally
they'd been taken to the hospital there. Her father had
been transferred to Dallas and had called Ethan, but
why? She couldn't imagine the reason he should have
asked a man he obviously disliked to look after his
daughter. She was no closer to solving the mystery when
the door opened.

Ethan came in with a cup of black coffee, looking
out of sorts, as if he'd never smiled in his life. He had a
faint arrogance of carriage that had intrigued her from
the first time she'd seen him. He was as individual as his
name. She even knew how he'd come by the name. His
mother Coreen, a John Wayne fan, had loved the movie
The Searchers, which came out before Ethan was born.
When Coreen became pregnant, she couldn't think of
a better name for her firstborn son than the first name
John Wayne had been given in the movie. So he became
Ethan Hardeman. His middle name was John, but few
people outside the family knew it.

Arabella loved looking at him. He had a rodeo rider's
physique, powerful shoulders and chest that wedged
down to narrow hips, a flat belly and long, muscular legs.
His face wasn't bad, either. He was tanned and his eyes
were deep-set and very gray, although sometimes they
looked silver and other times they had the faintest hint
of blue. His hair was dark and conventionally cut. His
nose was straight, his mouth sensuous, his cheekbones

high and his chin faintly jutting with a slight cleft. He had lean hands with long fingers and neatly trimmed flat nails.

She was staring at him again, helplessly, she supposed. From his blue-checked Western shirt to his gray denims and black boots, he was impeccably dressed, elegant for a cowboy, even if he was the boss.

"You look like hell," he said, and all her romantic dreams were pushed aside at once.

"Thank you," she replied with a little of her old spirit. "That kind of flattery is just what I needed."

"You'll mend." He sounded unruffled; he always did. He sat down in the armchair next to the bed and leaned back with one long leg crossed over the other, sipping his coffee. "Mother and Mary will be in to see you later. How's the hand?"

"It hurts," she said simply. She used the good one to brush back her hair. She could hear Bach preludes and Clementi sonatinas in the back of her mind. Always the music. It gave her life, made her breathe. She couldn't bear to think that she might lose it.

"Have they given you anything?"

"Yes, just a few minutes ago. I'm a little groggy, but I don't hurt as much as I did," she assured him. She'd already seen one orderly run for cover when he walked in. All she needed was to have Ethan bulldoze any more of the staff on her behalf.

He smiled faintly. "I won't cause too much trouble," he assured her. "I just want to make sure you're being treated properly."

"So does the staff," she murmured dryly, "and I hear at least two doctors are thinking of resigning if I'm not released soon."

He looked the least bit uncomfortable. "I wanted to make sure you got the best care possible."

"I did, never fear." She averted her eyes. "From one enemy to another, thanks for the TLC."

He stiffened. "I'm not your enemy."

"No? We didn't part as friends all those years ago." She leaned back, sighing. "I'm sorry things didn't work out for you and Miriam, Ethan," she said quietly. "I hope it wasn't because of anything I said…"

"It's past history," he said curtly. "Let it drop."

"Okay." He intimidated her with those black stares.

He sipped his coffee, allowing his eyes to wander down the length of her slender body. "You've lost weight. You need a rest."

"I haven't been able to afford that luxury," she told him. "We've only begun to break even this year."

"Your father could get a job and help out," he said coldly.

"You don't have the right to interfere in my life, Ethan," she said, staring back at him. "You gave that up years ago."

The muscles in his face contracted, although his gaze didn't waver. "I know better than you do what I gave up." He stared her down and drank some more coffee. "Mother and Mary are fixing up the guest room for you," he told her. "Matt's off at a sale in Montana, so Mary will be glad of the company."

"Doesn't your mother mind having me landed on her?"

"My mother loves you," he said. "She always has, and you've always known it, so there's no need to pretend."

"Your mother is a nice person."

"And I'm not?" He studied her face. "I've never tried to win any popularity contests, if that's what you mean."

She shifted against the pillows. "You're very touchy these days, Ethan. I wasn't looking for ways to insult you. I'm very grateful for what you've done."

He finished his coffee. His gray eyes met hers and for an instant, they were held against their will. He averted his gaze instantly. "I don't want gratitude from you."

That was the truth; not gratitude or anything else—least of all love.

She let her eyes fall to her hand in its cast. "Did you call the hospital at Dallas to ask about my father?"

"I phoned your uncle early this morning. The eye specialist is supposed to see your father today; they're more optimistic than they were last night."

"Did he ask about me?"

"Of course he asked about you," Ethan replied. "He was told about your hand."

She stiffened. "And?"

"He didn't say another word, according to your uncle." Ethan smiled without humor. "Well, what did you expect? Yours hands are his livelihood. He's just seen a future that's going to require him to work for a living again. I expect he's drowning in self-pity."

"Shame on you," she snapped.

He stared at her, unblinking. "I know your father. You do, too, despite the fact that you've spent your life protecting him. You might try living your own way for a change."

"I'm content with my life," she muttered.

His pale eyes caught and held hers, and he was very still. The room was so quiet that they could hear the sound of cars outside the hospital, in the nearby streets of Jacobsville.

"Do you remember what you asked me when they brought you in?"

She shook her head. "No. I was hurting pretty badly just then," she lied, averting her eyes.

"You asked if I remembered the swimming hole."

Her cheeks went hot. She pleated the material of the hospital gown they'd put her in, grimacing. "I can't imagine why I'd ask such a question. That's ancient history."

"Four years isn't ancient history. And to answer the question belatedly, yes, I remember. I wish I could forget."

Well, that was plain enough, wasn't it? she thought, hurt. She couldn't bring herself to meet his gaze. She could imagine the mockery in his eyes. "Why can't you?" she asked, trying to sound as unconcerned as he did. "After all, you told me yourself that I'd asked for it, that you'd been thinking about Miriam."

"Damn Miriam!" He got up, upsetting the coffee cup in the process, splattering a few drops of scalding coffee onto his hand. He ignored the sting, turning away to stare out the window at Jacobsville, his body rigid. He lifted the cup to his lips and sipped the hot liquid again to steady himself. Even the mention of his ex-wife made him tense, wounded him. Arabella had no idea of the hell Miriam had made of his life, or why he'd let her trap him into marriage. It was four years too late for explanations or apologies. His memories of the day he'd made love to Arabella were permanent, unchanged, a part of him, but he couldn't even tell her that. He was so locked up inside that he'd almost forgotten how to feel, until Arabella's father had telephoned him to tell him that Arabella had been injured. Even now, he could taste the sick fear he'd felt, face all over again the possibility that she might have died. The world had gone black until he'd gotten to the hospital and found her relatively unhurt.

"Do you hear from Miriam anymore?" she asked.

He didn't turn around. "I hadn't since the divorce was final, until last week." He finished the coffee and laughed coldly. "She wants to talk about a reconciliation."

Arabella felt her heart sink. So much for faint hope, she thought. "Do you want her back?"

Ethan came back to the bedside, and his eyes were blazing with anger. "No, I don't want her back," he said. He stared down at her icily. "It took me years to talk her into a divorce. Do you really think I have any plans to put my neck in that noose again?" he asked.

"I don't know you, Ethan," she replied quietly. "I don't think I ever did, really. But you loved Miriam once," she added with downcast eyes. "It's not inconceivable that you could miss her, or want her back."

He didn't answer her. He turned and dropped back down into the armchair by the bed, crossing his legs. Absently he played with the empty coffee cup. Loved Miriam? He'd wanted her. But love? No. He wished he could tell Arabella that, but he'd become too adept at keeping his deepest feelings hidden.

He put the cup down on the floor beside his chair. "A cracked mirror is better replaced than mended," he said, lifting his eyes back to Arabella's. "I don't want a reconciliation. So, that being the case," he continued, improvising as he began to see a way out of his approaching predicament, "we might be able to help each other."

Arabella's heart jumped. "What?"

He stared at her, his eyes probing, assessing. "Your father raised you in an emotional prison. You never tried to break out. Well, here's your chance."

"I don't understand."

"That's obvious. You used to be better at reading between the lines." He took a cigarette from the pack in his pocket and dangled it from his fingers. "Don't worry, I won't light it," he added when he saw the look she gave him. "I need something to do with my hands. What I meant was that you and I can pretend to be involved."

She couldn't prevent the astonished fear from distorting her features. He'd pushed her out of his life once, and now he had the audacity to want her to pretend to be involved with him? It was cruel.

"I thought you'd be bothered by the suggestion," he said after a minute of watching her expression. "But think about it. Miriam won't be here for another week or two. There's time to map out some strategy."

"Why can't you just tell her not to come?" she faltered.

He studied his boot. "I could, but it wouldn't solve the problem. She'd be dancing in and out of my life from now on. The best way, the only way," he corrected, "is to give her a good reason to stay away. You're the best one I can think of."

"Miriam would laugh herself sick if anyone told her you were involved with me," she said shortly. "I was only eighteen when you married her. She didn't consider me any kind of competition then, and she was right. I wasn't, and I'm not." She lifted her chin with mangled pride. "I'm talented, but I'm not pretty. She'll never believe you see anything interesting about me."

He had to control his expression not to betray the sting of those words. It hurt him to hear Arabella talk so cynically. He didn't like remembering how badly he'd had to hurt her. At the time, it didn't seem that he'd had a choice. But explaining his reasoning to Arabella four years too late would accomplish nothing.

His eyes darkened as he watched Arabella with the old longing. He didn't know how he was going to bear having to let her walk out of his life a second time. But at least he might have a few weeks with her under the pretext of a mutual-aid pact. Better that than nothing. At least he might have one or two sweet memories to last him through the barren years ahead.

"Miriam isn't stupid," he said finally. "You're a young woman now, well-known in your field and no longer a country mouse. She won't know how sheltered you've been, unless you tell her." His eyes slid gently over her face. "Even without your father's interference, I don't imagine you've had much time for men, have you?"

"Men are treacherous," she said without thinking. "I offered you my heart and you threw it in my teeth. I haven't offered it again, to anyone, and I don't intend to. I've got my music, Ethan. That's all I need."

He didn't believe her. Women didn't go that sour over a youthful infatuation, especially when it was mostly physical to begin with. Probably the drugs they'd given her had upset her reasoning, even if he'd give an arm to believe she'd cared that much. "What if you don't have music again?" he asked suddenly.

"Then I'll jump off the roof," she replied with conviction. "I can't live without it. I don't want to try."

"What a cowardly approach." He said the words coldly to disguise a ripple of real fear at the way she'd looked when she said that.

"Not at all," she contradicted him. "At first it was my father's idea to push me into a life of concert tours. But I love what I do. Most of what I do," she corrected. "I don't care for crowds, but I'm very happy with my life."

"How about a husband? Kids?" he probed.

"I don't want or need either," she said, averting her face. "I have my life planned."

"Your damned father has your life planned," he shot back angrily. "He'd tell you when to breathe if you'd let him!"

"What I do is none of your concern," she replied. Her green eyes met his levelly. "You have no right whatsoever to talk about my father trying to dominate me, when you're trying to manipulate me yourself to help you get Miriam out of your hair."

One silvery eye narrowed. "It amazes me."

"What does?" she asked.

"That you hit back at me with such disgusting ease and you won't say boo to your father."

"I'm not afraid of you," she said. She laced her fingers together. "I've always been a little in awe of my father. The only thing he cares about is my talent. I thought if I got famous, he might love me." She laughed bitterly. "But it didn't work, did it? Now he thinks I may not be able to play again and he doesn't want anything to do with me." She looked up with tear-bright eyes. "Neither would you, if it wasn't for Miriam hotfooting it down here. I've never been anything but a pawn where men were concerned, and you think my *father* is trying to run my life?"

He stuck the hand that wasn't holding the cigarette into his pocket. "That's one miserable self-image you've got," he remarked quietly.

She looked away. "I know my failings," she told him. She closed her eyes. "I'll help you keep Miriam at bay, but you won't need to protect me from my father. I very much doubt if I'll ever see him again after what's happened."

"If that hand heals properly, you'll see him again." Ethan tossed the unlit cigarette into an ashtray. "I have to get Mother and Mary and drive them in to see you. The man I sent for your clothes should be back by then. I'll bring your things with us."

"Thank you," she said stiffly.

He paused by the bedside, his eyes attentive. "I don't like having to depend on other people, either," he said. "But you can carry independence too far. Right now, I'm all you've got. I'll take care of you until you're back on your feet. If that includes keeping your father away, I can do that, too."

She looked up. "What do you have in mind to keep Miriam from thinking our relationship is a sham?"

"You look nervous," he remarked. "Do you think I might want to make love to you in front of her?"

Her cheeks went hot. "Of course not!"

"Well, you can relax. I won't ask you for the ultimate sacrifice. A few smiles and some hand-holding ought to get the message across." He laughed bitterly as he looked down at her. "If that doesn't do it, I'll announce our engagement. Don't panic," he added icily when he saw the expression on her face. "We can break it off when she leaves, if we have to go that far."

Her heart was going mad. He didn't know what the thought of being engaged to him did to her. She loved him almost desperately, but it was obvious that he had no such feeling for her.

Why did he need someone to help him get Miriam to leave him alone? she wondered. Maybe he still loved Miriam and was afraid of letting her get to him. Arabella closed her eyes. Whatever his reason, she couldn't let him know how she felt. "I'll go along, then," she said. "I'm so tired, Ethan."

"Get some rest. I'll see you later."

She opened her eyes. "Thank you for coming to see me. I don't imagine it was something you'd have chosen to do, except that Dad asked you."

"And you think I care enough for your father's opinion to make any sacrifices on his behalf?" he asked curiously.

"Well, I don't expect you to make any on mine," she said coolly. "God knows you disliked me enough in the old days. And still do, I imagine. I shouldn't have said anything to you about Miriam—"

She was suddenly talking to thin air. He was gone before the words were out of her mouth.

Ethan was back with Coreen and Mary later that day, but he didn't come into the room.

Coreen, small and delicate, was everything Arabella would have ordered in a custom-made mother. The little woman was spirited and kind, and her battles with Ethan were legendary. But she loved Arabella and Mary, and they were as much her daughters as Jan, her own married daughter who lived out of state.

"It was a blessing that Ethan was home," Coreen told Arabella while Mary, Arabella's best friend in public school, sat nearby and listened to the conversation with twinkling brown eyes. "He's been away from home every few days since his divorce was final, mostly business trips. He's been moody and brooding and restless. I found it amazing that he sent Matt on his last one."

"Maybe he was out making up for lost time after the divorce was final," Arabella said quietly. "After all, he was much too honorable himself to indulge in anything indecent while he was technically married."

"Unlike Miriam, who was sleeping with anything in pants just weeks after they married," Coreen said bluntly. "God knows why she held on to him for so long, when everyone knew she never loved him."

"There's no alimony in Texas," Mary grinned. "Maybe that's why."

"I offered her a settlement," Coreen said, surprising the other two women. "She refused. But I hear that she met someone else down in the Caribbean and there are rumors that she may marry her new man friend. That's more than likely why she agreed to the divorce."

"Then why does she want to come back?" Arabella asked.

"To make as much trouble as she can for Ethan, probably," Coreen said darkly. "She used to say things to him that cut my heart out. He fought back, God knows, but even a strong man can be wounded by ceaseless ridicule and humiliation. My dear, Miriam actually seduced a man at a dinner party we gave for

Ethan's business associates. He walked in on them in his own study."

Arabella closed her eyes and groaned. "It must have been terrible for him."

"More terrible than you know," Coreen replied. "He never really loved her and she knew it. She wanted him to worship at her feet, but he wouldn't. Her extramarital activities turned him off completely. He told me that he found her repulsive, and probably he told her, too. That was about the time she started trying to create as many scandals as possible, to embarrass him. And they did. Ethan's a very conventional man. It crushed him that Miriam thought nothing of seducing his business associates." Coreen actually shuddered. "A man's ego is his sensitive spot. She knew it, and used it, with deadly effect. Ethan's changed. He was always quiet and introverted, but I hate what this marriage has done to him."

"He's a hard man to get close to," Arabella said quietly. "Nobody gets near him at all now, I imagine."

"Maybe you can change that," Coreen said, smiling. "You could make him smile when no one else could. You taught him how to play. He was happier that summer four years ago than he ever was before or since."

"Was he?" Arabella smiled painfully. "We had a terrible quarrel over Miriam. I don't think he's ever forgiven me for the things I said."

"Anger can camouflage so many emotions, Bella," Coreen said quietly. "It isn't always as cut-and-dried as it seems."

"No, it isn't," Mary agreed. "Matt and I hated each other once, and we wound up married."

"I doubt if Ethan will ever marry anyone again," Arabella said, glancing at Coreen. "A bad burn leaves scars."

"Yes," Coreen said sadly. "By the way, dear," she said then, changing the subject, "we're looking forward to having you with us while you recuperate. Mary and I will enjoy your company so much."

Arabella thought about what Coreen had said long after they left. She couldn't imagine a man as masculine as Ethan being so wounded by any woman, but perhaps Miriam had some kind of hold on him that no one knew about. Probably a sensual one, she thought miserably, because everyone who'd seen them together knew how attracted he'd been to Miriam physically. Miriam had been worldly and sophisticated. It was understandable that he'd fallen so completely under her spell. Arabella had been much too innocent to even begin to compete for him.

A nurse came in, bearing a huge bouquet of flowers, and Arabella's eyes glistened with faint tears at their beauty. There was no card, but she knew by the size and extravagance of the gift that it had to be Coreen. She'd have to remember to thank the older woman the next day.

It was a long night, and she didn't sleep well. Her dreams were troubled, full of Ethan and pain. She lay looking up at the ceiling after one of the more potent dreams, and her mind drifted back to a late-summer's day, with the sound of bees buzzing around the wildflowers that circled the spot where the creek widened into a big hole, deep enough to swim in. She and Ethan had gone there to swim one lazy afternoon....

She could still see the butterflies and hear the crickets

and July flies that populated the deserted area. Ethan had driven them to the creek in the truck, because it was a long and tiring walk in the devastating heat of a south Texas summer. He'd been wearing white trunks that showed off his powerful body in an all-too-sensuous way, his broad shoulders and chest tapering to his narrow hips and long legs. He was deeply tanned, and his chest and flat belly were thick with curling dark hair. Seeing him in trunks had never bothered Arabella overmuch until that day, and then just looking at him made her blush and scamper into the water.

She'd been wearing a yellow one-piece bathing suit, very respectable and equally inexpensive. Her father's job had supported them frugally, and she was working part-time to help pay her tuition at the music school in New York. She was on fire with the promise of being a superb pianist, and things were going well for her. She'd come over to spend the afternoon with his sister Jan, but she and her latest boyfriend had gone to a barbecue, so Ethan had offered to take her swimming.

The offer had shocked and flattered Arabella, because Ethan was in his mid-twenties and she was sure his taste didn't run to schoolgirls. He was remote and unapproachable most of the time, but in the weeks before they went swimming together, he'd always seemed to be around when she visited his sister. His eyes had followed Arabella with an intensity that had disturbed and excited her. She'd loved him for so long, ached for him. And then, that day, all her dreams had come true when he'd issued his casual invitation to come swimming with him.

Once he'd rescued her from an overamorous would-be suitor, and another time he'd driven her to a school party along with Jan and Matt and Mary. To everyone's surprise, he'd stayed long enough to dance one slow, lazy dance with Arabella. Jan and Mary had teased her about it mercilessly. That had started the fantasies, that one dance. Afterwards, Arabella had watched Ethan and worshipped him from afar.

Once they were at the swimming hole, the atmosphere had suddenly changed. Arabella hadn't understood the way Ethan kept looking at her body, his silver eyes openly covetous, thrilling, seductive. She'd colored delicately every time he glanced her way.

"How do you like music school?" he'd asked while they sat in the grass at the creek's edge, and Ethan quietly smoked a cigarette.

She'd had to drag her eyes away from his broad chest. "I like it," she said. "I miss home, though." She'd played with a blade of grass. "I guess things have been busy for you and Matt."

"Not busy enough," he'd said enigmatically. He'd turned his head and his silver eyes had cut at her. "You didn't even write. Jan worried."

"I haven't had time. I had so much to catch up on."

"Boys?" he questioned, his eyes flickering as he lifted the cigarette to his thin lips.

"No!" She averted her face from that suddenly mocking gaze. "I mean, there hasn't been time."

"That's something." He'd crushed out the cigarette in the grass. "We've had visitors. A film crew, doing a commercial of all things, using the ranch as a backdrop. The models are fascinated by cattle. One of them actually asked me if you really pumped a cow's tail to get milk."

She laughed delightedly. "What did you tell her?"

"That she was welcome to try one, if she wanted to."

"Shame on you, Ethan!" Her face lit up as she stared at him. Then, very suddenly, the smile died and she was looking almost straight into his soul. She shivered with the feverish reaction of her body to that long, intimate look, and Ethan abruptly got to his feet and moved toward her with a stride that was lazy, graceful, almost stalking.

"Trying to seduce me, Bella?" he'd taunted softly, all too aware of how her soft eyes were smoothing over his body as he stopped just above her.

She'd really colored then. "Of course not!" she'd blurted out. "I was…just looking at you."

"You've been doing that all day." He'd moved then, straddling her prone body so that he was kneeling with her hips between his strong thighs. He'd looked at her, his eyes lingering on her breasts for so long that they began to feel tight and swollen. She followed his gaze and found the nipples hard and visible under the silky fabric. She'd caught her breath and lifted her hands to cover them, but his steely fingers had snapped around her wrists and pushed them down beside her head. He'd leaned forward to accomplish that, and now his hips were squarely over hers and she could feel the contours of his body beginning to change.

Her shocked eyes met his. "Ethan, what are you…" she began huskily.

"Don't move your hips," he said, his voice deep and soft as he eased his chest down over hers and began to drag it slowly, tenderly, against her taut nipples. "Lock your fingers into mine," he whispered, and still that aching, arousing pressure went on and on. He bent, so that his hard, thin mouth was poised just above hers. He bit softly at her lower lip, drawing it into his lips, teasing it, while his tongue traced the moist inner softness.

She moaned sharply at the intimacy of his mouth and his body, her eyes wide-open, astonished.

"Yes," he said, lifting his face enough to see her eyes, to hold them with his glittering ones. "You and me. Hadn't you even considered the possibility while you were being thrown at one eligible man after another by Jan's ceaseless matchmaking a few months ago?"

"No," she confessed unsteadily. "I thought you wouldn't be interested in somebody my age."

"A virgin has her own special appeal," he replied. "And you are still a virgin, aren't you?"

"Yes," she managed, wondering at her inability to produce anything except monosyllables while Ethan's body made hers ache all over.

"I'll stop before we do anything risky," he said quietly. "But we're going to enjoy each other for a long, long time before it gets to that point. Open your mouth when I kiss it, little one. Let me feel your tongue touching mine…"

She did moan then, letting his tongue penetrate the soft recesses of her mouth. The intimacy of it lifted her body against his and he made a deep, rough sound in his throat as he let his hips down over hers completely.

He felt her faint panic and subdued it with soft words and the gentle caress of his lean, strong hands on her back. Under her, the soft grass made a tickly cushion while she looked up into Ethan's quiet eyes.

"Afraid?" he asked gently. "I know you can feel how aroused I am, but I'm not going to hurt you. Just relax. We can lie together like this. I won't lose control, even if you let me do what comes next."

She felt the faint tenderness of her lips as she spoke, tasted him on them with awe. "What…comes next?" she asked.

"This." He lifted up on one elbow and traced his fingers over her shoulder and her collarbone, down onto the faint swell of her breast. He stroked her with the lightest kind of touch, going close to but never actually touching the taut nipple. She couldn't help her own reaction to the intimate feel of his lean fingers on her untouched body. She shuddered with pure pleasure, and the silver eyes above her watched with their own pleasure in her swift response.

"I know what you want," he whispered softly, and holding her gaze, he began to tease the nipple with a light, repetitive stroke that made her arch with each exquisite movement. "Have you ever done this with a man?"

"Never," she confessed jerkily. She shivered all over and her fingers bit into his muscular arms.

His face changed at her admission. It grew harder and his eyes began to glow. He lifted himself away a few inches. "Pull your bathing suit down to your hips," he said with rough tenderness.

"I couldn't!" she gasped, flushing.

"I want to look at you while I touch you," he said. "I want to show you how intimate it is to lie against a man's body with no fabric in the way to blunt the sweetness of touching."

"But, I've never…" she protested weakly.

His voice, when he spoke, was slow and soft and solemn. "Bella, is there another man you want this first time to be with?"

That put it all in perspective. "No," she said finally. "I couldn't let anyone else look at me. Only you."

His chest rose and fell heavily. "Only me," he breathed. "Do it."

She did, amazed at her own abandon. She pulled the straps gingerly down her arms and loosened the fabric from her breasts. His eyes slid down with the progress of the bathing suit and when she was nude from the waist up, he hung there above her, just looking at the delicate rise of her hard-tipped breasts, drinking in their beauty.

She gasped and his eyes lifted to hers, as they shared the impact of the first intimate thing they'd ever done together.

"I didn't think it would be you, the first time," she whispered shakily.

"That makes us even," he replied. His hand moved, tracing around her breast. His hips shifted, and she felt his pulsating need with awe as she registered his blatant masculinity.

His hand abruptly covered her breast, his palm taking in the hard nipple, and she moaned as his mouth ground down into hers.

Her body was alive. It wanted him, needed him. She felt her hips twist instinctively upward, seeking an even closer contact. He groaned, and one long, powerful leg insinuated itself between hers, giving her the contact she wanted. But it wasn't enough. It was fever, burning, blistering, and she felt her hands go to his hips, digging in, her voice breaking under the furious crush of his mouth. His hands slid under her, his hair-roughened chest dragged over her soft breasts while his hips thrust down rhythmically against hers and she felt him in a contact that made her cry out.

The cry was what stopped him. He had to drag his mouth away. She saw the effort it took, and he stared down at her with eyes that were frankly frightening. He was barely able to breathe. He groaned out loud. Then he'd arched away from her and gotten jerkily to his feet, to dive headfirst into the swimming hole, leaving a dazed, shocked Arabella on the bank with her bathing suit down around her hips.

She'd only just managed to pull it up when he finally climbed out of the water and stood over her. She was at a definite disadvantage, but she let him pull her to her feet.

He didn't let go of her hand. His fingers lifted it to his mouth, and he put his lips to its soft palm. "I envy the man who gets you, Bella," he said solemnly. "You're very special."

"Why did you do that?" she asked hesitantly.

He averted his eyes. "Maybe I wanted a taste of you," he said with a cynical smile before he turned away from her to get his towel. "I've never had a virgin."

"Oh."

He watched her gather up her own things and slip into her shoes as they went back to the pickup truck. "You didn't take that little interlude seriously, I hope?" he asked abruptly as he held the door open for her.

She had, but the look on his face was warning her not to. She cleared her throat. "No, I didn't take it seriously," she said.

"I'm glad. I don't mind furthering your education, but I love my freedom."

That stung. Probably it was meant to. He'd come very

close to losing control, and he didn't like it. His anger had been written all over his face.

"I didn't ask you to further my education," she'd snapped.

And he'd smiled, mockingly. "No? It seemed to me that you'd done everything but wear a sign. Or maybe I just read you too well. You wanted me, honey, and I was glad to oblige. But only to a certain point. Virgins are exciting to kiss, but I like an experienced woman under me in bed."

She'd slapped him. It hadn't been something she meant to do, but the remark had stung viciously. He hadn't tried to slap her back. He hadn't said anything. He'd smiled that cold, mocking, arrogant smile that meant he'd scored and nothing else mattered. Then he'd put her in the truck and driven her home.

The next week he'd been seen everywhere with Miriam, and Arabella overheard Miriam telling the other model about her plans for Ethan. Arabella had gone straight to Ethan, despite their strained relationship, to tell him what Miriam had said before it was too late. But he'd laughed at her, accused her of being jealous. And then he'd sent her out of his life with a scorching account of her inadequacies.

Four years ago, and she could still hear every word. She closed her eyes. She wondered if his memories were as bitter and as painful as her own. She doubted it. Surely Miriam had left him with some happy ones.

Finally, worn out and with her wounds reopened, she slept.

Chapter Three

The house Ethan and his family called home was a huge two-story Victorian. Set against the softly rolling land of south Texas, with cattle grazing in pastures that seemed to stretch forever, it was the very picture of an old-time Western movie set. Except that the cattle in their fenced pastures were very real, and the fences were sturdy and purposeful, not picture-perfect and overly neat. Jacobsville was within an easy drive of Houston, and Victoria was even closer. It had a small-town atmosphere that Arabella had always loved, and she'd known the people who lived there most of her life. Like the Ballenger brothers, who ran the biggest feedlot in the territory, and the Jacobs—Tyler and Shelby Jacobs Ballenger—whose ancestor the town was named for.

The elegant old mansion with its bone-white walls

and turret and gingerbread latticework was beautiful enough to have been featured in lifestyle magazines from time to time. It contained some priceless antiques both from early Texas and from England, because the first Hardeman had come over from London. The Hardemans were old money. Their fortune dated to an early cattle baron who made his fortune in the latter part of the nineteenth century during a blizzard that wiped out half the cattle ranches in the West. Actually, in the beginning, the family name had been Hartmond, but owing to the lack of formal education of their ancestor, the name was hopelessly misspelled on various documents until it became Hardeman.

Ethan looked like the portrait of that earlier Hardeman that graced the living-room mantel. They were probably much the same personality type, too, Arabella thought as she studied Ethan over the coffee he'd brought to the guest room for her. He was a forbidding-looking man with a cool, very formal manner that kept most people at arms' length.

"Thank you for letting me come here," she said.

He shrugged. "We've got plenty of room." He looked around the high ceiling of the room she'd been given. "This was my grandmother's bedroom," he mused. "Remember hearing Mother talk about her? She lived to be eighty and was something of a hell-raiser. She was a vamp or some such thing back during the twenties, and *her* mother was a died-in-the-wool suffragette. One of the bloomer girls, out campaigning for the vote for women."

"Good for her." Arabella laughed.

"She'd have liked you," he said, glancing down at her. "She had spirit, too."

She sipped her coffee. "Do I have spirit?" she mused. "I let my father lead me around by the nose my whole life, and I guess I'd still be doing it if it hadn't been for the accident." She glanced at the cast on her wrist, sighing as she juggled the coffee mug in one hand. "Ethan, what am I going to do? I won't even have a job, and Daddy always took care of the money."

"This is no time to start worrying about the future," he said firmly. "Concentrate on getting well."

"But—"

"I'll take care of everything," he interrupted. "Your father included."

She put the coffee mug down and lay back against the pillows. Her wrist was still uncomfortable and she was taking pain capsules fairly regularly. She felt slightly out of focus, and it was so nice to just lie there and let Ethan make all the decisions.

"Thank you, Ethan," she said and smiled up at him.

He didn't smile back. His eyes slid over her face in an exploration that set all her nerves tingling. "How long has it been since you've had any real rest?" he asked after a minute.

She shifted on the pillows. "I don't know. It seems like forever." She sighed. "There was never any time." Her stomach muscles clenched as she remembered the constant pressure, the practice that never stopped, the planes and motel rooms and concert halls and recording dates and expectant audiences. She felt her body going rigid with remembered stress as she recalled how she'd had to force herself more and more to go out on the stage, to keep her nerve from shattering at the sight of all those people.

"I suppose you'll miss the glamour," Ethan murmured.

"I suppose," she said absently and closed her eyes, missing the odd look that passed over his dark face.

"You'd better get some sleep. I'll check on you later."

The bed rose as he got up and left the room. She didn't even open her eyes. She was safe here. Safe from the specter of failure, safe from her father's long, disapproving face, safe from the cold whip of his eyes. She wondered if he was ever going to forgive her for failing him, and decided that he probably wouldn't. Tears slid down her cheeks. If only he could have loved her, just a bit, for what she was underneath her talent. He'd never seemed to love her.

Coreen sat with her for most of the day. Ethan's little mother was a holy terror when she was upset, but everyone loved her. She was the first person in the door when someone was sick or needed help, and the last to leave. She gave generously of her time and money, and none of her children had a bad word to say about her, even in adulthood. Well, except Ethan, and sometimes Arabella thought he did that just for amusement because he loved to watch his mother throw things in a temper.

Arabella had seen the result of one memorable fight between mother and son, back during her teenage years when she was visiting Ethan's brother and sister with Mary. Arabella, Mary, Jan and Matt had been playing

Monopoly on the living-room floor when Ethan and his mother got into it in the kitchen. The voices were loud and angry, and unfortunately for Ethan, his mother had been baking a cake when he provoked her. She threw a whole five-pound bag of flour at him, followed by an open jar of chocolate syrup. Arabella and Mary and Jan and Matt had seen Ethan walk by, covered from Stetson hat to booted feet in white flour and chocolate syrup, leaving a trail of both behind him on the wooden floor as he strode toward the staircase.

Arabella and the others had gaped at him, but one cold-eyed look in their direction dared them to open their mouths. Arabella had hidden behind the sofa and collapsed in silent laughter while the others struggled valiantly to keep straight faces. Ethan hadn't said a word, but Coreen had continued to fling angry insults after him from the kitchen doorway as he stomped upstairs to shower and change. For a long time afterward, Arabella had called him, "the chocolate ghost." But not to his face.

Coreen was just a little over five foot three, with the dark hair all her children had inherited, but hers was streaked with silver now. Only Ethan shared her gray eyes. Jan and Matt had dark blue eyes, like their late father.

"Do you remember when you threw the flour at Ethan?" Arabella asked, thinking aloud as she watched Coreen's deft fingers working a crochet hook through a growing black-and-red afghan.

Coreen looked up, her plump face brightening. "Oh, yes, I do," she said with a sigh. "He'd refused to sell that bay gelding you always liked to ride. One of my best friends wanted him, you see, and I knew you'd be away at music school in New York. He wasn't a working horse." She chuckled. "Ethan dug in his heels and then he gave me that smile. You know the one, when he knows he's won and he's daring you to do anything about it. I remember looking at the open flour sack." She cleared her throat and went back to work on the afghan. "The next thing I knew, Ethan was stomping down the hall leaving a trail of flour and chocolate syrup in his wake, and I had to clean it up." She shook her head. "I don't throw things very often these days. Only paper or baskets—and nothing messy."

Arabella smiled at the gentle countenance, wishing deep in her heart that she'd had a mother like Coreen. Her own mother had been a quiet, gentle woman whom she barely remembered. She'd died in a wreck when Arabella was only six. Arabella didn't remember ever hearing her father talk about it, but she recalled that he'd become a different man after the funeral.

She twisted her fingers in the blue quilted coverlet. Her father had discovered by accident that Arabella had a natural talent for the piano, and he'd become obsessed with making her use it. He'd given up his job as a clerk in a law office, and he'd become a one-man public relations firm with his daughter as his only client.

"Don't brood, dear," Coreen said gently when she saw the growing anguish on Arabella's lovely face. "Life is easier when you accept things that happen to you and just deal with them as they crop up. Don't go searching for trouble."

Arabella looked up, shifting the cast with a wince because the break was still tender. They'd taken out the clamps that had held the surgical wound together before they put on the cast, but it still felt as if her arm had been through a meat grinder.

"I'm trying not to," she told Ethan's mother. "I thought my father might have called, at least, since they put me back together. Even if it was just to see if I had a chance of getting my career back."

"Being cynical suits my son. It doesn't suit you," Coreen said, glancing at her over the small reading glasses that she wore for close work. "Betty Ann is making a cherry cobbler for dessert."

"My favorite," Arabella groaned.

"Yes, I know, Ethan told us. He's trying to fatten you up."

She frowned at the older woman. "Is Miriam really trying to come back to him?"

With a long-suffering sigh, Coreen laid the afghan and crochet hook over her knees. "I'm afraid so. It's the last thing in the world he needs, of course, after the way she cut up his pride."

"Maybe she still loves him," Arabella suggested.

Coreen cocked her head. "Do you know what I think? I think she's just lost her latest lover and he's left her pregnant. She'll try to lure Ethan into bed and convince him it's his child, so that he'll take her back."

"You really should write books," Arabella said dryly. "That's a great plot."

Coreen made a face at her. "Don't laugh. I wouldn't put it past her. She isn't as pretty as she used to be. All that hard living and hard drinking have left their mark on her. One of my friends saw her on a cruise recently, and Miriam was pumping her for all sorts of information about Ethan—if he'd remarried or was keeping company with anyone."

"He wants me to keep company with him," Arabella mentioned, "to keep Miriam at bay."

"Is that what he told you?" Coreen smiled gently. "I suppose it's as good an excuse as any."

"What do you mean?" Arabella asked curiously.

Coreen shook her head. "That's for Ethan to tell you. Are you going to keep company with him?"

"It seems little enough to do for him, when he's kind enough to give me a roof over my head and turn the whole household upside down on my account," she said miserably. "I feel like an intruder."

"Nonsense," Coreen said easily. "We all enjoy having you here, and none of us wants Miriam to come back. Do play up to Ethan. It will turn Miriam green with envy and send her running."

"Is she going to stay here?" Arabella asked worriedly.

"Over my dead body," Ethan drawled from the doorway, staring across the room at Arabella.

"Hello, dear. Been rolling in the mud with the horses again?" Coreen asked pleasantly.

He did look that way, Arabella had to admit. He was wearing working gear—chambray shirt, thick denims, weathered old leather chaps, boots that no self-respecting street cowboy would have touched with a stick, and a hat that some horse had stepped on several times. His dark skin had a thin layer of dust on it, and his work gloves were grasped in one lean hand that didn't look much cleaner.

"I've been doctoring calves," he replied. "It's March," he reminded her. "Roundup is in full swing, and we're on the tail end of calving. Guess who's going to be nighthawking the prospective mamas this week?"

"Not Matt," Coreen groaned. "He'll leave home!"

"He needs to," Ethan said imperturbably. "He and Mary can't cuss each other without an audience around here. It's going to affect their marriage sooner or later."

"I know," Coreen said sadly. "I've done my best to persuade Matt that he can make it on his own. God knows, he can afford to build a house and furnish it on his income from those shares Bob left him."

"We're too good to him," Ethan pointed out. "We need to start refusing to speak to him and putting salt in his coffee."

"If you put salt in my coffee, I'd stuff the cup up your…" Coreen began hotly.

"Go ahead," Ethan said when she hesitated, his pale eyes sparkling. "Say it. You won't embarrass me."

"Oh, I'll drink to that," Coreen murmured. "You're too much my son to be embarrassed."

Arabella looked from one to the other. "You do favor each other," she said. "Your eyes are almost exactly the same shade."

"He's taller," Coreen remarked.

"Much taller, shrimp," he agreed, but he smiled when he said it.

Coreen glared at him. "Did you come up here for any particular reason, or do you just enjoy annoying me?"

"I came to ask Arabella if she wanted a cat."

Arabella gaped at him. "A what?"

"A cat," he repeated. "Bill Daniels is out front with a mother cat and four kittens that he's taking to the vet to be put down."

"Yes, I want a cat," Arabella said at once. "Five cats."

She gnawed her lower lip. "God knows what my father will say when he finds out, though. He hates cats."

"Why not think about what *you* want for a change, instead of what your father wants?" Ethan asked curtly. "Or have you ever had your own way?"

"Once, he let me have chocolate ice cream when he told me to get vanilla," she replied.

"That isn't funny," Ethan said darkly.

"Sorry." She leaned back against the pillows. "I guess I've never tried to stand up to him." It was the truth. Even though she'd rebelled from time to time, her father's long-standing domination had made it difficult for her to assert herself. Incredible, when she thought nothing of standing up to Ethan…

"No time like the present. I'll tell Bill we'll keep the cats." He moved away from the doorjamb. "I've got to get back to work."

"Like that?" Coreen asked. "You'll embarrass your men. They won't want to admit they work for someone as filthy as you are."

"My men are even filthier than I am," he replied proudly. "Jealous because you're clean?"

Coreen moved her hand toward the trash basket, but Ethan just smiled and left the room.

"You wouldn't have thrown it at him, would you?" Arabella asked.

"Why not?" Coreen asked. "It doesn't do to let men get the upper hand, Bella. Especially not Ethan," she added, looking at Arabella thoughtfully. "You've learned that much, I see. Ethan is a good man, a strong man. But that's all the more reason to stand up to him. He wants his own way, and he won't give an inch."

"Maybe that was one reason he and Miriam couldn't make a go of it."

"That, and her wild ways. One man just wasn't enough for her," Coreen replied.

"I can't imagine anyone going from Ethan to someone else," Arabella said. "He's unique."

"I think so, even if he is my son." Coreen picked up her afghan and her crochet hook. "How do you feel about him, Bella?"

"I'm very grateful to him for what he's done for me," she said evasively. "He's always been like a big brother…."

"You don't have to pretend," Coreen said gently. "I'm perceptive, even if I don't look it." She lowered her eyes to her crocheting. "He made the mistake of his life by letting you get away. I'm sorry for both of you that it didn't work out."

Arabella studied the coverlet under her nervous hands. "It's just as well that it didn't," she replied. "I have a career that I hope to go back to. Ethan…well, maybe he and Miriam will patch things up."

"God forbid," Coreen muttered. She sighed wearily. "Life goes on. But I'm glad Ethan brought you home with him, Bella." She looked up. "He isn't a carefree man, and he takes on too much responsibility sometimes. He's forgotten how to play. But he changes when he's with you. It makes me happy to see how different he is when you're around. You always could make him smile."

Arabella thought about that long after Coreen had gone downstairs to help Betty Ann in the kitchen. Ethan did smile more with her than he did with other people. He always had. She'd noticed it, but it surprised her that his mother had.

For two days, Arabella was confined to bed against her will. Doctor's orders, they told her, because she'd been concussed and badly bruised in the wreck. But on the third day, the sun came out and the temperature was unnaturally high that afternoon for early March. She got downstairs by herself, a little wobbly from her enforced leisure, and sat down in the porch swing.

Coreen had gone to a ladies' circle meeting and Mary was shopping, so there was no one to tell her she couldn't go outside. Mary had helped her dress that morning in a snap-front, full denim skirt and a long-sleeved blue sweatshirt. She'd tied her hair back with a blue velvet ribbon. She looked elegant even in such casual attire, and the touch of makeup she'd used made her look more alive. Not that anyone would be around to notice.

And that was where she was mistaken. The pickup truck pulled into the yard and Ethan got out of it, pausing on the steps when he saw her sitting in the swing.

"Who the hell told you to get out of bed?" he demanded.

"I'm tired of staying in bed," she replied. Her heart went wild just at the sight of him. He was wearing faded jeans and a chambray shirt with a beat-up, tan Stetson, and his boots were muddy as he joined her on the porch. "It's a beautiful day," she added hopefully.

"So it is." He lit a cigarette and leaned against the post, his pale eyes lancing over her. "I checked with your uncle this morning."

"Did you?" She watched him curiously.

"Your father left Dallas for New York this morning." His eyes narrowed. "Do you know why?"

She grimaced. "The bank account, I guess. If there's anything in it."

"There's something in it," he said pleasantly enough. "But he won't get to it. I had my attorney slap an injunction on your father, and the bank has orders not to release a penny to him. That's where I've been."

"Ethan!"

"It was that or have him get you by the purse strings," he said quietly. "When you're back on your feet again, you can play twenty questions with him. Right now, you're here to get well, not to have yourself left penniless by your mercenary father."

"Do I have much?" she asked, dreading the answer, because her father had enjoyed a luxurious lifestyle.

"You have twenty-five thousand," he replied. "Not a fortune, but it will keep you if it's invested properly."

She stared at his muscular arms, remembering the strength of them. "I didn't think ahead," she said. "I let him put the money in a joint account because he said it was the best way. I guess I owe you my livelihood, don't I?" she added with a smile.

"You're earning it," he replied quietly.

"By helping you get rid of Miriam," she agreed.

"We'll have to do a little work on you first," he returned. He studied her for a long moment. "You washed your hair."

"Actually, Mary and I washed my hair. I have to get Mary to help me dress with this thing on," she muttered, holding up the arm with the cast and then grimacing at the twinge of pain it caused. "I can't even fasten my bra—" She bit off the rest of the word.

His eyes narrowed. "Embarrassed to talk about undergarments with me?" he asked. "I know what women wear under their clothes." He grew suddenly distant and cold. "I know all too well."

"Miriam hurt you very badly, didn't she, Ethan?" she asked without meeting his eyes. "I suppose having her come back here makes all the scars open up again." She looked up then, catching the bitterness in his expression before he could erase it.

He sighed heavily and lifted the cigarette to his lips with a vicious movement of his fingers. He stared out over the horizon blankly. "Yes, she hurt me. But it was my pride, not my heart, that took a beating. When I threw her out, I vowed that no woman was going to get a second shot at me. So far, no one has."

Was he warning her off? Surely he knew that she'd never have the courage to set her cap for him again. He'd knocked her back hard enough over Miriam.

"Well, don't look at me," she said with a forced smile. "I'm definitely not Mata Hari material."

Some of the tenseness left him. He stubbed out the finished cigarette in an ashtray nearby. "All the same, little one, I can't see you sleeping around. Before or after marriage."

"We go to church," she said simply.

"I go to church myself."

She clasped her hands in her lap. "I read about this poll they took. It said that only four percent of the people in the country didn't believe in God."

"The four percent that produce motion pictures and television programs, no doubt," he muttered dryly.

She burst out laughing. "That was unkind," she said. "They aren't atheists, they're just afraid of offending somebody. Religion and politics are dangerous subjects."

"I've never worried about offending people," Ethan replied. "In fact, I seem to have a knack for it."

She smiled at him. He made her feel alive and free, as if she could do anything. Her green eyes sparkled as they met and held his silver ones, and the same electricity ran between them that had bound them together, years ago, one lazy day in late summer. The look had been translated into physical reality that one time, but now it only made Arabella sad for something she'd never have again. Even so, Ethan didn't look away. Perhaps he couldn't, she thought dazedly, feeling her heart shake her with its beat, her body tingle all over with sweet, remembered pleasure.

He said something rough under his breath and abruptly turned away. "I've got to get down to the holding pens. If you need anything, sing out. Betty Ann's in the kitchen."

He left without a backward glance.

Arabella stared after him with open longing. It seemed that she couldn't breathe without setting him off. And even if he could have felt something for her, he wasn't going to let his guard down again. He'd already said so. Miriam had really done a job on his pride.

She leaned back in the swing and started it swinging. Odd that he hadn't found someone to replace Miriam as soon as his marriage was over. He could have had his pick on looks alone, never mind the fortune behind his name. But he'd been a loner ever since, from what Mary had said. Surely Miriam couldn't have hurt him that much—unless he was still in love with her.

She sighed. She was a little afraid of Ethan. She was much too vulnerable and he was close at hand and alone. Ironically, Miriam's arrival might be her only hope of keeping her heart from being broken by him all over again.

Chapter Four

Arabella had supper with the family for the first time that night, and Matt announced that he was taking Mary to the Bahamas for a much-needed vacation.

"Vacation?" Ethan glared at him. "What's that?"

Matt grinned. He looked a lot like his brother, except that he had deep blue eyes and Ethan's were silver. Matt was shorter, less formidable, but a hard worker in spite of his easygoing nature.

"A vacation is a thing I haven't had since I got married. I'm leaving and Mary is going with me."

"It's March," Ethan pointed out. "Calving? Round-up...?"

"I never asked for a honeymoon," Matt replied with an eloquent glance.

Ethan and Coreen exchanged wry looks. "All right.

Go ahead," Ethan told him dryly. "I'll just have an extra set of arms put on and manage without you."

"Thanks, Ethan," Mary said gently. Her eyes glanced shyly off his and she smiled at her husband with pure delight.

"Where in the Bahamas did you plan to go?" Ethan asked.

Matt grinned. "That's a secret. If you don't know where I am, you can't look for me."

Ethan glared at him. "I tried that four years ago. You found me."

"That was different," Matt said. "A note came due at the bank and they wouldn't let me arrange the renewal."

"Excuses, excuses," Ethan replied.

"You might look at houses before you come back," Coreen murmured.

Matt shook his finger at her. "Not nice."

"Just a thought," she replied.

"If we leave, who'll save you from Ethan?" Matt asked smugly.

Arabella glanced at Ethan, who looked more approachable tonight than he had since she'd come home from the hospital. She felt suddenly mischievous. She raised her hand. "I volunteer."

Ethan's silvery eyes lanced her way with faint surprise and a little delight in them as he studied her face. "It'll take more than you, cupcake," Ethan said, and he smiled.

The smile reminded her of what Coreen had said, about how easily Ethan had once smiled for Arabella. The knowledge went to her head. She wrinkled her nose at him. "I'll recruit help. At least one of the cowboys was offering to spray you with malathion late this afternoon. I heard him."

"He was offering to spray *me* with insecticide?" Ethan glowered. "Which cowboy?" he demanded, with a look that meant trouble for the man.

"I won't tell. He might come in handy later," Arabella returned.

"Feeling better, are we?" Ethan murmured. He lifted an eyebrow. "Watch out. We'll get in trouble."

Arabella looked around. "I thought there was only one of me."

Ethan felt frankly exhilarated, and that disturbed him. He had to drag his eyes away from Arabella's soft face. He stared at his brother instead. "Why don't you want a house of your own?" Ethan asked him.

"I can't afford one."

"Horsefeathers," Ethan muttered. "You've got a great credit rating."

"I don't like the idea of going that deep in debt."

Ethan sat back in his chair and chuckled. "You don't know what debt is until you spend ninety thousand dollars for a combine."

"If you think that's high for a harvesting machine, just consider the total cost of tractors, hay balers and cattle trailers," Coreen added.

"I know, I know," Matt conceded. "But you're used to it. I'm not. Mary's applied for a job at the new textile plant that just opened. They're looking for secretarial help. If she gets it, we might take the plunge. But first we take a vacation. Right, honey?"

"Right," Mary said eagerly.

"Suit yourself," Ethan said. He finished his coffee and stood up. "I've got to make a couple of phone calls."

Involuntarily, his eyes were drawn to Arabella. She looked up in time to meet that searching gaze, and a long, static moment passed during which Ethan's jaw clenched and Arabella flushed.

Arabella managed to look away first, embarrassed even though Coreen and the others were engaged in conversation and hadn't noticed.

Ethan paused by her chair and his lean hand went to her dark hair, lightly brushing it. He was gone before she could question whether it had been accidental or deliberate. Either way, her heart went wild.

She spent the evening listening to Matt and Mary talk about their planned trip, and when bedtime came, she was the first to go up. She was on the bottom step of the staircase when Ethan came out of his study and joined her there.

"Come here, little one, I'll carry you up." He bent, swinging her gently into his arms, careful of the hand that was in the cast.

"It's my arm, not my leg," she stammered.

He started up the stairs, easily taking her weight. He glanced down at her. "I don't want you to overdo it."

She was silent, and he drank in the feel of her in his arms. He'd never managed to forget how she felt close against him, and he'd tried, for years. Of course she didn't need to be carried. But he needed to carry her, to feel her body against him, to bring back the bittersweet memories of the one time he'd made love to her. It had haunted him ever since, especially now that she was here, in his house. He hardly slept at all these days, and when he did, his dreams were full of her. She didn't know that, and he wasn't going to admit it. It was much too soon.

She felt her breath whispering out at the concern in his deep voice. She couldn't think of anything to say. She curled her arms hesitantly around his neck and nuzzled her face into his shoulder. His breath caught and his step faltered for an instant, as if her soft movement had startled and disturbed him.

"Sorry," she whispered.

He didn't answer. He'd felt something when she moved that way. Something that he hadn't felt in a long time. His arms tightened as he savored the warm weight of Arabella's body, the faint scent of flowers that clung to her dark hair.

"You've lost weight," he said as he reached the landing.

"I know." Her breasts rose and fell in a gentle sigh, bringing them into a closer, exciting contact with his chest. "Aren't you glad? I mean, if I weighed twice as much as I do, you might pitch headfirst down the stairs and we'd both wind up with broken necks."

He smiled faintly. "That's one way of looking at it." He shifted her as he reached her bedroom, edging through the doorway. "Hold tight while I close the door."

She did, shivering a little at his closeness. He felt that betraying tremble and stopped dead, lifting his head to look into her wide, bright eyes with a heart-stopping intensity.

"You like being close to me, don't you?" he asked. His senses stirred with a sensuality that he hadn't felt in years.

Arabella went scarlet. She dropped her eyes and went rigid in his arms, struggling for something to say.

Amazingly, her embarrassment intensified the excitement he was feeling. It was like coming to life after being dead. His body rippled with desire and he felt like a man for the first time in four years. He kicked the door shut and carried her to the bed. He tossed her onto it gently and stood over her, his eyes lingering on the soft thrust of her breasts. His eyes darted back up to catch hers, his heart feeding on the helpless desire he found on her face.

So she hadn't forgotten, any more than he had. For one wild minute, he thought about going down beside her, arching his body over her own and kissing her until she gasped. But he moved away from the bed before his body could urge him on. Arabella might want him, but her virginal state was enough of a brake for both of them. She was still bitter about the past, and what he was feeling might not last. He had to be sure….

He lit a cigarette, repocketing his lighter roughly.

"I thought you'd quit, until this afternoon," Arabella said, sitting up. She was uncomfortable with the silence and his sudden withdrawal. Why had he taunted her with that intimate remark and then looked as if she'd asked him to do it? Shades of the past, she thought.

"I had quit until you got yourself banged up in that wreck," he agreed with a cold glance. "That started me back."

"So did having a flat tire in the truck." She began to count off the reasons on one hand. "There was the time the men got drunk the night before roundup started. Then there was the day your horse went lame. And once, a horse bit you…."

"I don't have to have excuses to smoke," he reminded her. "I've always done it and you've always known it." His eyes narrowed as he studied her soft face. "I was smoking that day by the creek. You didn't complain about the taste of it when I kissed you."

She felt the sadness that must have been reflected in her eyes. "I was eighteen," she said. "A couple of boys had kissed me, but you were older and more worldly." She lowered her eyes. "I was trying so hard to behave like a sophisticated woman, but the minute you touched me, I went to pieces." She sighed heavily. "It seems like a hundred years ago. I guess you were right, too; I did throw myself at you. I was besotted with you."

He had to struggle not to go to her, to pull her into his arms and kiss the breath out of her. She felt guilty, when he was the one who'd been wrong. He'd hurt her. He'd wounded her pride, just as Miriam had wounded his, and sent her running. Perhaps her father would never have gotten such a hold on her if he'd told Miriam to go to hell and asked Arabella to marry him.

"What tangled webs we weave," he said quietly. "Even when we aren't trying to deceive people."

"You couldn't help loving Miriam," she replied.

His face froze. Amazing how just the sound of his ex-wife's name could turn him off completely. He lifted the cigarette to his mouth, the hardness in him almost brittle as he stared down at Arabella.

Arabella watched him. "Do you realize how you look when someone mentions her, Ethan?" she asked gently.

"I realize it," he said curtly.

"And you don't want to talk about it. All right, I won't ask," she replied. "I can imagine she dealt your pride a horrible blow. But sometimes all it takes to repair the damage is having your ego built back up again."

His pale eyes pierced hers, and the look they exchanged was even more electric and intimate than the one downstairs.

"Are you offering to give me back my self-esteem?" he asked.

Years seemed to pass while she tried to decide if he meant that question. He couldn't have, she decided finally. He'd made it clear four years ago just how he felt. She shivered. "No, I'm not offering anything, except to give a good performance when Miriam gets here," she told him. "I owe you that much for taking me in while I get well."

His eyes blazed. "You owe me nothing," he said coldly.

"Then I'll do it for old times' sake," she returned with icy pride. "You were like the big brother I never had. I'll do it to pay you back for looking out for me."

He felt as if she'd hit him. The only thing that gave him any confidence was the way she'd reacted to being in his arms. He blew out a cloud of smoke, staring at her with total absorption. "Any reason will do," he said. "I'll see you in the morning."

He turned and started toward the door.

"Well, what do you want me to say?" she burst out. "That I'd do anything you asked me to do short of murder? Are you looking for miracles?"

He stopped with his hand on the doorknob and looked at her. "No, I'm not looking for miracles." He searched her face. Somewhere inside, he felt dead. "I put the cat and kittens in the barn," he said after a minute. "If you'd like to see them, I'll take you down there in the morning."

She hesitated. It was an olive branch of sorts. And if they were going to convince Miriam, they couldn't do it in a state of war. She moved restlessly on the bed. "Yes, I'd like that. Thank you."

"De nada," he said in careless Spanish, a habit because of the Mexican vaqueros who worked for him, who still understood their own language best. Ethan spoke three or four languages fluently, which often surprised visitors who felt his Texas drawl indicated a deprived education.

She watched him leave with pure exasperation. He kept her so confused and upset that she didn't know if she was coming or going.

Mary and Matt left the next morning. Arabella hugged Mary goodbye, feeling a little lost without her best friend. Ethan's new outlook and the specter of Miriam's approach seemed daunting, to say the least.

"Don't look so worried," Mary said gently. "Ethan and Coreen will take good care of you. And Miriam won't be staying here. Ethan wouldn't have it."

"I hope you're right. I have a feeling Miriam could take skin off with words."

"I wouldn't doubt that," Mary replied, grimacing. "She can be nasty, all right. But I think you might be equal to her, once you got going. You used to be eloquent when you lost your temper. Even Ethan listened." She laughed.

"I haven't had much practice at losing my temper, except with Ethan," Arabella replied. "Wish me luck."

"I will, but you won't need it, I'm sure," Mary said.

Ethan drove them to the airport in Houston so they wouldn't have to take the shuttle flight out of Jacobsville airport. But he was back before Arabella expected him, and he hadn't forgotten about the kittens.

"Come on, if you're still interested." He took her good hand, tugging her along with him, not a trace of emotion showing on his face.

"Shouldn't we tell your mother where we're going?" she protested.

"I haven't told my mother where I was going since I was eight," he said shortly. "I don't need her permission to walk around the ranch."

"I didn't mean it that way," she muttered.

It did no good at all. He ignored her. He was still wearing what he called his city clothes, charcoal slacks with a pale blue shirt and a Western-cut gray-and-black sport jacket.

"You'll get dirty," she said as they entered the wide-aisled barn.

He glanced down at her. "How?"

She could have made a joke about it with a less intimidating man, but not with Ethan. This unapproachable man would have cut her to pieces.

"Never mind." She moved ahead of him, neatly dressed herself in a pair of designer jeans and a pale yellow pullover that would show the least hint of dirt.

She walked down the aisle and went where he gestured, feeling his presence with fear and delight. It was sobering to think that but for the accident that had damaged her hand, she might never have seen Ethan again.

Her hand. She glanced down at it, seeing the helplessness of it emphasized by the cast. Threads of music drew through her mind. She could hear the keys, feel the chords, the melody, the minors, the subdominants....

She closed her eyes and heard Clementi's *Sonatina,* its

three movements one of the first pieces she'd mastered when she began as an intermediary student. She smiled as it was replaced in her thoughts by the exquisite *English Suite* by Bach, and *Finlandia* by Grieg.

"I said, here are the kittens. Where were you?" Ethan asked quietly.

She opened her eyes, and realized as she did that her fingers might never feel those notes again. She might never be able to play a melody in more than a parody of her former ability. Even the pop tunes would be beyond her. She'd have no way to support herself. And she certainly couldn't expect her father to do it, not when he wouldn't even phone or come near her. At least Ethan had managed to save some of her earnings, but they wouldn't last long if her father hadn't paid off the debts.

There was panic in her eyes, in her pale face.

Ethan saw it. He tapped her gently on the nose, the antagonism dying out of him all at once when he saw her tormented expression. He had to stop baiting her. It wasn't her fault that Miriam had crippled him as a man. "Stop trying to live your life all at one time. There's nothing to panic about."

Her eyes met his. "That's what you think."

"Let tomorrow take care of itself." He went down on one knee. "Now, this is worth seeing."

He gestured for her to kneel down beside him, and all her cares were lost in the magic of five snow-white, newborn kittens. Their mother, too, was a snow-white shorthair with deep blue eyes.

"Why, I've never seen a cat like this!" she exclaimed. "A white cat with blue eyes!"

"They're pretty rare, I'm told. Bill found them in his barn, and he's not a cat fancier."

"And they were going to be put to sleep." She groaned. "I'll rent them an apartment if my father gives me any trouble," she said firmly. She smiled at the mother cat and then looked longingly at the kittens. "Will she let me hold one?"

"Of course. Here." He lifted a tiny white kitten and placed it gently in Arabella's hand, which she held close to her body to make sure it didn't fall. She nuzzled its tiny head with her cheek, lost in the magic of the new life.

Ethan watched her, his eyes indulgent and without mockery. "You love little things, don't you?"

"I always have." She handed back the kitten with obvious reluctance, taking the opportunity to stroke it gently. "I always thought that one day I'd get married and have children, but there seemed to be one more concert, one more recording date." She smiled wistfully. "My father was determined to make sure that I never had the chance to get serious about anyone."

"He couldn't risk losing you." Ethan put the kitten back down, stroking the mother's head gently before he rose, bringing Arabella up with him. He brushed back her long, loose dark hair with both hands. Then, in the silence of the barn, which was only broken by an occasional movement or sound from the horses nearby, his hands moved to frame her face. "I used to take you riding. Remember?"

"Yes. I haven't been on a horse since. Ethan, why wouldn't you let your mother sell the horse I used to ride here?" she asked suddenly, remembering what Coreen had said about it.

He shifted restlessly. "I had my reasons."

"And you won't tell me what they were?"

"No." He searched her eyes slowly, hungrily. He felt his heartbeat increasing as the nearness of her began to affect him, just as it had the night before. "It's been a hell of a long time since you and I have been alone together," he said quietly.

She lowered her eyes to his broad chest, watching its heavy rise and fall. "Years," she agreed nervously.

He touched her hair gently, trailing it through his fingers, feeling the silkiness of it. "Your hair was long, then, too," he recalled, catching her soft eyes. "I pillowed you on it in the grass when we made love by the old swimming hole."

Her heart went wild. It was all she could do to hold on to her self-control. "We didn't make love," she said through her teeth. "You kissed me a few times and made sure I didn't take it seriously. It was to 'further my education,' didn't you say?"

"You were grass-green and stupid about men," he said curtly. "You felt my body against yours. You may have been a kid then, but you sure as hell ought to know by now how dangerous the situation was getting when I called a halt."

"It doesn't make any difference now," she said miserably. "As I said, you made sure I didn't take it seriously. I was just being my usual stupid self. Now can we go back to the house?"

He slid his hands roughly into her hair and held her face up to his pale, glittering eyes. "You were eighteen," he said shortly. "A virginal eighteen with a father who hated my guts and had complete control of your life.

Only a heartless fool would have seduced you under those circumstances!"

She stared at him, shocked by the fury in his eyes, his voice. "And you were nobody's fool," she agreed, almost shaking with mingled fear and hurt. "But you don't have to pretend that you cared about my feelings, not after the things you said to me…!"

His hands contracted and he drew in a sharp breath. "God in heaven, how can you be so blind?" he groaned. His gaze fell to her mouth and he drew her face up toward his, his lips parting. "I wanted you!"

The words went into her mouth. He was fitting his lips with exquisite slowness to her own in a silence thick with tense emotion. But even as his mouth brushed against hers, even as she felt the sharp intake of his breath and felt the pressure of his hands on her face, a sound broke the spell and froze him in place.

It was the loud roar of a car driving up outside. Ethan's head lifted abruptly and the look in his eyes was almost feverish. His hands had a faint tremor as he drew them away from her face, and he was breathing roughly. So was she. She felt as if her legs wouldn't even support her.

Her eyes asked the question she didn't dare.

"I've been alone a long time," he said curtly, and he gave her a mocking smile. "Isn't that what you'd like to believe?"

Before she could answer, he let go of her and turned toward the front of the barn.

"I'm expecting a buyer this morning," he said gruffly. "That must be him."

He went down the wide aisle ahead of her, almost grateful for the diversion. He'd lost his head just then, gotten drunk on the exquisite promise of Arabella's mouth under his. He hadn't realized how vulnerable he'd become since she'd been here. He was going to have to be more careful. Rushing her would accomplish nothing; he should be thankful that his buyer had interrupted.

But when he reached the yard, the visitor wasn't his buyer at all. It was a taxi, and getting out of the back seat, all leggy glamour and red lipstick, was Miriam Hardeman. If she wasn't going to be a houseguest, obviously nobody had thought to inform her of it, because the cabdriver was slowly getting six expensive suitcases out of the trunk of the car.

Ethan's face went stiff as Arabella joined him and he felt as if he were breaking out in a cold sweat. Miriam. Just the sight of his ex-wife was enough to shake his self-confidence to its foundations. He schooled his face to show nothing as he turned toward Arabella and held out his hand, silently commanding her cooperation, as she'd promised it.

Beside him, Arabella stared at the newcomer as if she were a particularly vicious disease. Which, in fact, was a fair analogy. She let Ethan's hand envelop hers and she held on for dear life. They were in it together now, for better or worse.

Chapter Five

Miriam raised a delicately etched eyebrow as Ethan and Arabella joined her. She stared hard at Arabella, almost incredulously, her eyes sharp and immediately hostile. She noticed that Ethan and the younger woman were holding hands, and for a minute, she seemed to lose a little of her poise. Then she smiled, almost as if by force of will, because there was no joy in her dark green eyes.

"Hello, Ethan." She tossed back her long auburn hair nervously. "I hope you got my telegram?"

He stared back at her, refusing to be taunted. "I got it."

"Pay the cabdriver, would you?" she persisted. "I'm flat broke. I hope you don't mind my staying here, Ethan, because I blew my last dollar on this outfit and I just can't afford a hotel."

Ethan didn't say a word, but his expression grew even more remote.

Arabella watched Ethan pay the driver, then her eyes darted to Miriam. The woman was perfection itself. Flaming red highlights in her long auburn hair, dark green, witchy eyes, an exquisite face and figure. But she was showing her age a bit, and she was heavier than she had been. What Coreen had said about pregnancy came home with full force. Yes, Miriam could be pregnant, all right. That would explain that slight weight gain, mostly in her waist.

"Hello, Arabella," Miriam said as she studied the younger woman coldly. "I've heard enough about you over the years. I remember you, of course. You were only a child when Ethan and I married."

"I've grown up," Arabella said quietly. She stared after Ethan with soft longing. "At least, Ethan thinks so."

Miriam laughed haughtily. "Does he, really?" she asked. "I suppose a very young woman would appeal to him, since she wouldn't know what she was missing."

That was an unexpected taunt. Arabella didn't understand it, or the way Ethan looked when he came back, after gesturing for one of his passing cowboys to carry Miriam's luggage up to the house.

"Tell her why you won't get involved with experienced women, Ethan, dear," Miriam murmured sarcastically.

Ethan stared at her with the intimidating look that Arabella hated. It even seemed to work on Miriam.

"Arabella and I go back a long way. We were involved before you and I were, Miriam," he added, staring levelly at his ex-wife.

Miriam's eyes blazed. "Yes, I remember your mother saying that," she replied.

The expression on Miriam's face did Ethan more good than anything had in years. He drew Arabella close against his side, giving her a quick, pleased glance when she let her body go lax against him. "You weren't expected until next week," he told Miriam.

"I just finished a modeling assignment down in the Caribbean and I thought I'd stop by on my way back to New York," Miriam replied. She fidgeted with her purse, nervously it seemed.

Arabella stared at Miriam from the shelter of Ethan's hard arm. It was almost rigid around her, which told her plenty about how he was reacting to the woman's presence. She didn't understand the undercurrents. If he still loved Miriam, she didn't see why he couldn't just say it. Why this pretense, when Miriam was obviously still jealous of him?

"How long do you want to stay?" Ethan asked. "We're pretty busy right now and I hope you understand that Arabella and I consider our time together precious."

Miriam lifted an eyebrow. "How convenient that you should turn up just now, Arabella. You've been pursuing your career for several years, I believe?"

"Bella was injured in a wreck. Naturally I want her where I am," Ethan replied with a cool smile. "I hope you'll enjoy spending your evenings talking to Mother."

"I'll manage," Miriam said irritably. "Well, let's go up to the house. I'm tired and I want a drink."

"You won't drink here," Ethan said firmly. "We don't keep liquor in the house."

"Don't keep…!" Miriam gasped. "But we always had a full liquor cabinet!"

"You did," Ethan corrected. "When you left, I had the bottles thrown out. I don't drink."

"You don't do anything," Miriam said with a nasty inflection. "Especially in bed!" she lashed out.

Ethan's arm tightened around her. Arabella was beginning to catch on, or she thought she was. She felt her hair bristling as she stared at the older woman with pure fury. Ethan didn't need defending, and he'd probably be furious that she dared say anything, but this was too much! Miriam had run around on him; what did she expect when he was repulsed by it? Even love would have a hard time excusing that kind of hurt.

Ethan himself was having to bite his tongue. He knew how Miriam would love to provoke him into losing his temper, to give her an excuse to tell Arabella all their dark secrets. He didn't want that, not until he'd had time to tell her himself. His pride demanded that much.

But Arabella got in the first words, her face lifted proudly as she faced the older woman without flinching. "You may have had problems in bed," Arabella said quietly, clinging to Ethan's hand. "Ethan and I don't." Which was the gospel truth, but not the way Miriam took it. Ethan smothered a shocked gasp. He hadn't expected her to sacrifice her reputation for him, certainly not with such surprising courage.

Miriam shuddered with fury. "You little…!"

The word she'd used was dying on the air even as Ethan broke into it, his face fiercely angry at the way Arabella was trembling despite her brave front. "The road is that direction," Ethan indicated. "I'll send a cab after you. No way are you going to exercise your vicious tongue on my future wife!"

Miriam backed down immediately. Arabella didn't do anything; she was too shocked at being referred to as Ethan's future wife.

"I'm sorry," Miriam said on a swallowed breath. "I suppose I did lay it on with a trowel." She glanced at Ethan, curious and nervous now, unusually so. "I...I guess it shocked me to think you'd gotten over me."

"I meant what I said," he replied, his voice cutting. "If you stay here, it's on my terms. If I hear so much as one sharp word to Bella, off you go. Is that clear?"

"It had better be, isn't that what you mean, Ethan?" Miriam forced a smile. "All right, I'll be the perfect houseguest. I thought we were going to talk about a reconciliation."

"Perhaps you did," Ethan said calmly. "Bella and I are going to be married. There's no room in my life for you now or ever."

Miriam seemed to go pale. She straightened, elegant in her pale gray suit, and smiled again. "That's pretty blunt."

"Blunt is the only way to be with you," Ethan said. "After you," he said, standing aside to let her enter the house.

Arabella was still stunned, although she had the presence of mind to wonder if Miriam's outburst hadn't been prompted by fear rather than anger. Which made her wonder why Miriam was so afraid of having Ethan involved with another woman. Ethan took her hand in his, feeling its soft coldness.

"You're doing fine," he said quietly, so that Miriam couldn't hear. "Don't worry, I won't let her savage you."

"I didn't mean to say that…."

He smiled gently, despite his drawn features. "I'll explain it to you later."

"You don't have to explain anything to me," she said, her eyes level and unblinking. "I don't care what Miriam says."

He drew in a deep breath. "You're full of surprises."

"So are you. I thought you were going to save the engagement threat as a last resort," she murmured.

"Sorry. This seemed the best time. Come on. Chin up."

She managed a smile and, holding tight to his lean hand, followed him into the house.

Coreen was unwelcoming, but she was too much a lady to show her antagonism for Miriam outright. She camouflaged it behind impeccable manners and cold courtesy. The only time a smile touched her lips was when Ethan sat down close beside Arabella on the sofa and drew her against him with a possessive arm.

It had thrilled Arabella earlier when Ethan had defended her so fiercely. Perhaps it had just been his distaste for Miriam's manners, but it was nice to think that he cared enough to stand up for her. She curled up on the sofa against him, drinking in his nearness, loving the scent and feel of him so close. This was the one nice thing that had come out of Miriam's visit. Arabella could indulge her longing for Ethan without giving herself away. What a pity that he was only pretending, to keep Miriam from seeing how vulnerable he was.

She glanced up at him, watching his lean face as he listened with coolly polite interest to Miriam's monologue about her travels. He was so tense, and she felt that what Miriam had said about him in bed had hurt him. She remembered what Coreen had said about his finding Miriam repulsive and she wondered if that was what Miriam had been referring to. Odd that he'd gone so white at the reference. Well, a woman like that could do plenty of damage even to a strong man's pride. She had a vicious tongue and no tolerance for other people. It wasn't the kind of attitude that kept a marriage together, especially when she'd never given Ethan any kind of fidelity. That must have cut his heart to pieces, loving her as he had.

"What are you doing down here, Arabella?" Miriam asked eventually. "I thought you were in New York."

"I was touring," Arabella replied. "I was on my way back from a charity performance when the car was wrecked."

"She was coming back here," Ethan inserted smoothly with a warning glance at Arabella. "She'd gone with her father. I should have driven her myself."

Arabella let out an inaudible sigh at the way she'd almost slipped up. Miriam would hardly believe that she and Ethan were engaged if Arabella was living in New York and they never saw each other.

"Will you be able to use your hand again, or is your career up the creek?" Miriam asked with a pointed smile. "I guess Ethan wouldn't want you to do anything except have babies anyway."

"As I recall," Ethan said coldly, "you were quite emphatic about not wanting any. That was after I married you, of course," he added meaningfully.

Miriam shifted restlessly. "So I was. Is there anything to do around here? I hate television," she said, quickly changing the subject.

"Ethan and Arabella and I like to watch the nature

specials," Coreen said. "In fact, there's a fascinating program about polar bears on tonight, isn't there, dear?" she asked Ethan.

Ethan exchanged a glance with his mother. "There is, indeed."

Miriam groaned.

It was the longest day Arabella could remember. She managed to dodge Miriam by staying with Ethan, even when he went out to check on the roundup. He usually took a horse, but in deference to Arabella's injured wrist, he was driving the ranch pickup.

He glanced at her. "Doing okay?" he asked.

She smiled. "I'm fine, thanks." He'd changed out of his traveling clothes into his worn jeans and boots and a blue plaid Western-cut shirt. His wide-brimmed hat was tilted at a rakish angle over his forehead. He looked very cowboyish, and Arabella grinned at the thought.

"Something funny?" he asked with a narrow, suspicious gaze.

"I was just thinking how much like a cowboy you look," she replied. "Not bad, for the boss."

"I don't have to wear suits around the men to get their attention."

"I remember." She shuddered.

"Stop that." He took a draw from the smoking cigarette in his hand. "You were a surprise this morning," he said unexpectedly. "You handled Miriam very well."

"Did you expect me to break into tears and run for cover?" she asked. "I've had a lot of practice with bad-tempered people. I lived with my father, remember."

"I remember. Miriam's the one who ran for cover this time."

"You had a few bites of her, yourself. My gosh, what a

venomous woman!" she said huskily. "I don't remember her being that bad before."

"You didn't know her before. Or maybe you did," he added quietly. "You saw through her from the beginning."

She studied his averted face for a long moment, wanting to ask him something more, but uncertain of the way to go about it.

He sensed her curiosity and glanced toward her. "Go ahead. Ask me."

She started. "Ask you what?"

He laughed coldly as he drove the truck along the rough track beside the fence, bouncing them both in the seats even with the superior shocks under the truck body. "Don't you want to know why she was surprised when you gave her the impression we were lovers?"

"I thought she was just being sarcastic," she began.

He turned the truck and headed it toward another rutted path. Then abruptly he stopped it and cut off the engine. He had the windows down, and the sounds of birds and the distant bawling of cattle filtered in through it.

He sat with one hand on the steering wheel, the other holding the cigarette. He shifted in the seat and stared at Arabella fully, his silver eyes touching her face while he struggled with an explanation he didn't want to make. But Miriam was bound to say something to Arabella, and he wanted it to come from him, not from his venomous houseguest.

"Miriam took a lover two weeks after we were married," he said quietly. "There was a procession of them until I divorced her. She said that I couldn't satisfy her in bed."

He said it with icy bluntness, his eyes dark with pain, as if it were a reflection on his manhood. Perhaps it was. Arabella had read that a man's ego was the most vulnerable part of him.

She searched his face quietly. "It seems to me that nobody could satisfy her, Ethan. She certainly had a lot of lovers."

He didn't realize that he'd been holding his breath until then. Arabella's attitude took the sting out of the admission. He relaxed a little. "They say everything goes if both partners want it, but I was too old-fashioned to suit Miriam." He smoked his cigarette quietly.

She glanced at him. "Coreen thinks Miriam's pregnant and that's why she came back to try for a reconciliation. She wants to get you into bed and pretend it's yours."

"I told you at the outset, I don't want her," he said bluntly. "In bed or otherwise. She'd have to do a hell of a lot of pretending to get me to go along."

"She could tell people you were the father," she countered.

He sighed. "Yes, she probably could. That may be what she has in mind."

"What are we going to do?" she asked.

"I'll think of something," he said without looking at her. Locking his bedroom door might be the best answer, but wouldn't Miriam enjoy that, he thought bitterly.

"I could help if you'd tell me what to do," she replied. "All I know about sex is what you taught me that day," she added without looking at him.

That got his full attention. His breath was expelled in an audible rush. "My God," he said roughly. "You're kidding."

"I'm afraid not."

"Surely there were other men?"

"Not in the way you mean."

"You had to go out on dates in the past four years," he persisted. "You could be a virgin and still have some experience."

She'd backed herself into a corner now, she thought worriedly. How could she tell him that the thought of any other man's hands and eyes on her body had nauseated her? She looked for a way to change the subject.

"Answer me, Arabella," he said firmly.

She glared at him. "I won't."

He began to smile. "Was it so good with me that you didn't want it with anyone else?" he asked slowly. She blushed and averted her eyes, and he felt as if he were floating.

He reached out unexpectedly and caught a strand of her hair, savoring its silky softness. "I don't know how I managed to stop. You were extraordinarily responsive."

"I was infatuated with you," she replied. "I wanted so desperately to show you that I was grown up." She stared at his broad chest. "I suppose I did, but it didn't help. We'd at least been on relatively friendly terms until then."

He closed the ashtray and sat up straight again to study her through narrowed eyes. "I suppose you're right. If we're going to pull this off, you and I are going to have to give the appearance of intimacy when we're around Miriam," he said abruptly, changing the subject.

She was glad to return to the present. Discussion about the past was still unpleasant. "You mean, I need to wear low-cut dresses and slink when I walk and sit on your lap and curl your hair around my fingers? Especially in front of Miriam?"

"You're catching on, cupcake," he replied.

"It wouldn't embarrass you?" she asked with a faint grin.

"Well, as long as you don't try to take my clothes off in public," he said. It was the first trace of humor she'd noticed in him since Miriam came. "We wouldn't want to embarrass my mother."

"You'll have to settle for partial seduction right now, I'm afraid," she sighed, indicating her wrist in the cast. "It's hard enough undressing myself without having to undress you, too."

"That reminds me," he murmured with a pointed look at the straps under her blouse, "how do you manage to get undressed?"

She lifted her shoulders. "I can manage most everything. Except what's underneath."

"You might consider going without what's underneath for the duration of Miriam's stay," he suggested somberly. "I'll try not to stare, but it might give her food for thought if you walk around in front of me that way."

"Your mother will have a heart attack," she replied.

"Not my mother. She's been in your corner since you were eighteen." His eyes darkened as they searched hers. "She never could understand why I preferred Miriam to you."

"I could," she said with a harsh laugh. "Miriam was everything I wasn't. Especially sophisticated and experienced." She stared down at her lap with returning bitterness. "All I had going for me was a little talent. And now I may not even have that."

"None of that," he said curtly. His hand tightened around hers. "We won't think ahead. We won't think about when that cast comes off or your father's reaction. We'll think about Miriam and how to get her out of here. That's our first priority. You give me a hand and I'll do the same for you when your father shows up."

"Will he show up, Ethan?" she asked miserably.

The soft green eyes looking so trustingly into his made his pulse hammer in his throat. She was as pretty as she'd been at eighteen, and just as shyly innocent. He wouldn't have traded her tenderness for all of Miriam's glittery sophistication, but he no longer had that choice. Arabella was only playing a part in this mutual-protection pact. He couldn't lose sight of that fact. Arabella wasn't his. With the bitterness of the past between them, she probably never would be.

"It doesn't matter whether or not he does," he replied. He studied her long, elegant fingers. "I'll take care of you."

She felt little thrills down her spine. If only he meant it! She closed her eyes, drinking in the scent of his cologne, the warmth of his lean, powerful body so close to her.

There had been so little affection in her life. She'd been alone and unloved. Her father had only wanted her talent, not her company. No one had ever loved her, but she wanted Ethan to. She wanted him to care as much as she did. But that would never happen now. Miriam had killed what love there was in him.

"You're so quiet, little one," Ethan said. He tilted her chin up and searched her sad eyes. "What's wrong?"

The softness of his voice brought tears. They stung her eyelids and when she tried to hide them, he held her face firmly in both lean hands and made her look at him.

"Why?" he asked roughly.

Her lower lip trembled and she caught it in her teeth to still it. "It's nothing," she managed. Her eyes closed. She was a hopeless coward, she thought. She wanted to say why can't you love me, but she was afraid to.

"Stop trying to live your whole life in one day," he said sharply. "It won't work."

"I guess I worry too much," she confessed, brushing away a shiny tear from her cheek. "But everything's turned upside down. I had a promising career and a nice apartment in New York. I traveled…and now I may be a has-been. My father won't even talk to me," she faltered.

"He'll be in touch," he said. "Your hand will mend. Right now you don't need a job; you've already got one."

"Yes," she said with a weak smile. "Helping you stay single."

He gave her an odd look. "I wouldn't put it that way," he corrected. "The idea is to get Miriam to leave without bloodshed."

She lifted her face. "She's very beautiful," she said, searching his pale silver eyes. "Are you sure you don't want her back, Ethan? You loved her once."

"I loved an illusion," he said. His fingers brushed at a long strand of dark brown hair, moving it behind her ear. "Outward beauty isn't any indication of what's inside, Arabella. Miriam thought that beauty was enough, but a kind spirit and a warm heart mean a lot more to most people than a pretty face."

"She's not quite as cold as she was," she said.

He smiled faintly, searching her eyes. "Are you trying to push me into her arms?"

"No." She lowered her eyes to his hard mouth. "I just wondered if you were sure that getting rid of her is what you really want."

He drew her forehead against his chest, smoothing down her ruffled hair as he stared over her head and out the window. "I'm sure," he replied. "It wasn't much of a marriage to begin with." He drew back and looked at Arabella's soft face, drinking in its delicate beauty, its strength of character. "I wanted her," he said absently. "But wanting isn't enough."

Perhaps wanting was all he was capable of, though, Arabella thought miserably. He'd wanted her years ago, but he hadn't loved her. He said he hadn't loved Miriam, but since he married her, he must have felt something pretty powerful for her.

"What are you thinking about now?" he asked at her forehead.

"Just long thoughts," she confessed. She drew in a steadying breath and lifted a smile to show him. "I'm all—"

His mouth settled unexpectedly on hers, covering the word even as she spoke it.

She stiffened at the feel of his firm lips on hers. All the years since he'd touched her, and it was as if they'd never been apart. She remembered the scent of him, the way his mouth bit at hers to make it open just as it had the first time he'd ever kissed her. She remembered the sound he made in his throat when he dragged her face under his with rough, warm hands and the feverish intensity of the mouth that grew instantly more demanding and intimate on her lips.

"Kiss me," he whispered, his breath making little chills on her moist lips. "Don't hold back."

"I don't want this—" she protested with her last whisper of will.

"You want me. You always have and I've always known it," he said roughly.

His fingers speared into her long hair, tangling in its dark softness while his mouth crushed down on hers again, pressing her lips firmly apart as he began to build the intensity of the kiss from a slow possession to a devastating intimacy.

She stiffened and he hesitated, his mouth poised just above her own.

"Don't fight me," he said huskily. His hands moved, faintly tremulous where they held her face captive. He was burning. On fire for her. The old need was back, in full force, and she was his, if only for a space of seconds. He wanted her so desperately. She was his heart. Miriam and all the pain were forgotten in his driving hunger to hold Arabella's soft body in his arms, to feel again the aching sweetness of her mouth under his. "Oh, God, let me love you," he ground out.

"You don't," she said miserably. "You don't, you never did…!"

He took the words into his open mouth. He groaned heavily and his hands slid over her back, bringing her gently against him, so that her breasts flattened against his hard chest while he kissed her. Her hands pressed against his warm shirtfront, but she didn't kiss him back or put her arms around him. She was too afraid that he'd been stirred up by his ex-wife and now he needed an outlet. It was…demeaning.

He felt her lack of response and lifted his head. He could hardly breathe. His chest actually throbbed with the fierce thunder of his heart, and the sight of Arabella's flushed, lovely face under his made it go even faster. She looked frightened, although there was something under the fear, a leashed hunger that she was refusing to satisfy.

And that wasn't the only thing he noticed. Despite the blow Miriam had dealt his pride, he discovered that he was suddenly very much a man. He felt desire as he held Arabella; a raging desire he'd thought for four years he'd never be able to feel again for a woman. The impact of it brought a muffled curse from his lips. Of all the times for it to happen, and with Arabella, of all people!

Chapter Six

Arabella couldn't meet Ethan's searching gaze, and the faint tremor in his arms frightened her. He looked and felt out of control, and she knew the strength in that lean body. She tried to pull away, but he drew her even closer, his hard, dark face poised just above her own.

"What's wrong?" he asked roughly.

"You want Miriam," she said through numb lips. "You want her, and I'm substituting, all over again."

He was utterly shocked. His arms loosened and she took advantage of the momentary slackening to pull away from him. She couldn't bear the confinement of the cab a minute longer. She opened the door and climbed down, locking her arms around her breasts as she stared at the flat horizon and listened to the buzzing noise of insects in the heat of the day.

Ethan got out, too, lighting a cigarette. He walked

along beside her with apparent carelessness, steering her toward a grove of mesquite trees by the small stream that led eventually to the swimming hole. He leaned against the rough trunk of a huge mesquite tree, smoking quietly while Arabella leaned against a nearby tree and watched butterflies fluttering around a handful of straggly wildflowers on the creek bank.

The silence became unnerving. Ethan's eyes narrowed as he studied Arabella's slender body. "You weren't substituting for Miriam in the truck."

She colored, avoiding his level gaze. "Wasn't I?"

He took a draw from the cigarette and stared at the ripples in the water. "My marriage is over."

"Maybe she's changed," she said, rubbing salt in her own wounds. "It could be a second chance for you."

"Miriam's the one with the second chance," he returned, his cold eyes biting into her face. "To bring me to my knees. The only thing she ever saw in me was the size of my wallet."

And that was the most hurtful part of it, she imagined. He'd loved Miriam and all she'd wanted was his money. She rubbed her cast with a light finger, tracing patterns on it. "I'm sorry. I guess that was rough."

"No man likes being a walking meal ticket," he said shortly. He finished the cigarette and tossed it onto the ground, putting it out with a vicious movement of his boot.

"Then maybe she'll give up and go away," she said.

"Not if you don't help me give her the right impression about our relationship," he said curtly. He pushed away from the tree and walked toward her with somber intent in his pale eyes. "You said you'd need a little cooperation. All right. You'll get it."

"No, Ethan," she choked. Even in her innocence, she recognized the purposeful stride, the glitter in his enveloping gaze. It was the same look he'd had on his face that day at the swimming hole. "Oh, Ethan, don't! It's just a game to you. It's Miriam you want. It's always been Miriam, never me!"

He moved in front of her and his lean hands shot past her to the broad tree trunk, imprisoning her. He held her eyes relentlessly. "No," he said huskily. He searched her face and his heart went wild. Even his body, frozen though it had been for four long years, was alive as never before.

"Don't," she pleaded as her breath caught in her throat. The scent and feel of him was making her weak. She didn't want to be vulnerable again, she didn't want to be hurt. "Please don't."

"Look at me."

She shook her head.

"I said, look at me!"

The sheer force of will in the deep drawl brought her rebellious eyes up, and he trapped them.

Still holding her eyes with his, he lowered his body against hers, letting her feel the raging arousal she'd kindled.

Her eyes dilated. She could barely breathe. After one shocked minute, she tried to struggle, but he groaned and his eyes closed. He shuddered. She stood very still, her lips parted.

He looked down at her for a long time, his eyes dark with desire, his body rigid with it. "My God," he whispered almost reverently. "It's been so long…." His mouth ground into hers with fierce delight. He was a man again, whole again. He could hardly believe what he was feeling.

Arabella was drowning in him. His warm masculine body was making her ache terribly, but she couldn't afford to give in.

"I won't love you, Ethan," she whispered, her expression tormented as memories of the past wounded her. "I won't, I won't!"

His heart began to swell in his chest. So that was it. The secret fear. He smiled faintly, letting his gaze fall to her soft bow of a mouth as he began to realize how vulnerable she was, and why. "We'll take it one day at a time," he breathed as his head bent. "Do you remember how I taught you to kiss—with your teeth and your tongue as well as your lips?"

She did, but it wouldn't have mattered, because he was teaching her all over again. She felt the brush of his warm, hard lips over her own, felt them tug on her lower lip and then her upper lip, felt the soft tracing of his tongue between them and the gentle bite of his teeth as he coaxed her mouth to open and admit the slow, deliberate penetration of his tongue.

A sound escaped her tight throat. Her body stiffened under his. The fingers of her uninjured hand began to open and close, her nails making tiny scraping sensations even through his shirt to his throbbing chest.

"Open my shirt," he said into her mouth.

She hesitated and he kissed her roughly.

"Do it," he bit off against her lips. "You've never touched me that way. I want you to."

She knew it was emotional suicide to obey him, but her fingers itched to touch his warm, dark skin. She felt his lips playing gently against her mouth while she fumbled the buttons out of the buttonholes until, finally, her fingers could tangle in the thick dark growth of hair over his chest to find the warm, taut skin beneath it.

Unthinking, she drew back to look at where her fingers were touching, fascinated concentration in her soft green eyes as she registered the paleness of her long fingers against the darkness of his hair-matted skin.

"Put your mouth against me," he said unsteadily. "Here. Like this." He caught the back of her head and coaxed her face against him. She breathed in soap and cologne and pure, sweet man as her lips pressed softly where he guided them.

"Ethan?" she whispered uncertainly. This was unfamiliar territory, and she could feel that his body was rigid with desire. He was shuddering with it.

"There's nothing to be afraid of, Arabella," he said at her lips. "Let me lift you…God, baby!" he ground out, shuddering. His hips pinned hers to the tree, but she never felt the rough bark at her spine. Her arms went around him, both of them trembling as the intimate contact locked them together as forcefully as a blazing electric current.

She was crying with the sheer impact of it, her arms holding him even as his full weight came down against her.

"You can't get close enough to me, can you?" he groaned. "I know. I feel the same way! Move your legs, sweet…yes!"

His leg insinuated its powerful length between hers, intensifying the intimacy of the embrace.

"I want you." His hands caught her hips, moving them with slow, deliberate intent into his while his mouth probed hers. "I want you, Arabella. God, I want you so!"

She was incapable of answering him. She felt him pick her up, but her eyes were closed. She was his. Whatever he wanted, whatever he did, she had no desire to stop him.

She felt the wind in her hair and Ethan's mouth on hers. The strength of his arms absorbed the shock of his footsteps as he carried her back to the truck.

He opened the door and put her in the passenger seat, sliding her to the middle of the cab so that he could fit facing her, his eyes intent on her flushed face.

Arabella could hardly breathe for the enormity of what had just happened. She'd never expected Ethan to make such a heavy pass at her with Miriam in residence. But it was because of Miriam, she was sure of it. He just didn't want to admit that his heart was still in bondage to the woman he couldn't satisfy. Her eyes fell to his opened shirt, to the expanse of his muscular chest, and lingered there.

"Nothing to say?" he asked quietly.

She shook her head slowly.

"I won't let you pretend that it didn't happen." He tilted her face up to his. "We made love."

Her cheeks went scarlet. "Not…not quite."

"You wouldn't have stopped me." He traced her lower lip with a long, teasing forefinger. "Four years, and the intensity hasn't lessened. We touch each other and catch fire."

"It's just physical, Ethan," she protested weakly.

He caught her long hair in his hands and drew it around her throat. "No."

"Miriam's here and you're frustrated because she didn't want you…."

He lifted an eyebrow. "Really?"

She folded the arm in the cast and stared at it. "Shouldn't we go back?"

"You were the one asking for cooperation," he reminded her.

"Was that why you kissed me?" she ventured.

"Not really." He brushed his lips over her eyes, closing her eyelids gently. "You make me feel like a man," he whispered huskily. "I'm whole again, with you."

She didn't understand that. He'd said that he couldn't satisfy Miriam, but he was certainly no novice. She was shaking from the intensity of his lovemaking.

"What are you going to do about tonight?" She tried to change the subject. "Miriam will surely make a beeline for your bedroom."

"Let me handle Miriam," he said. "Are you sure you want to go home?"

She wasn't, but she nodded.

He framed her face in his lean hands and made her look at him. "If your body was all I wanted, I could have had it four years ago," he reminded her gently. "You would have given yourself to me that day at the swimming hole."

Her lips parted on a rush of breath. "I don't understand."

"That's obvious." He kissed her roughly and let her go, climbing down out of the cab. He shut the door, went around to get in himself, and started the truck with a jerky motion of his fingers.

"You said it was just to get rid of Miriam, that we'd pretend to be involved," she began dazedly.

He glanced at her, his pale eyes approving the swell of her mouth, the faint flush of her cheeks. "But we weren't pretending just now, were we?" he asked quietly. "I said we'd take it one day at a time, and that's how it's going to be. Just let it happen."

"I don't want to have an affair," she whispered.

"Neither do I." He put the truck in gear and pulled back into the ruts, bouncing them over the pasture. "Light this for me, honey."

He handed her a cigarette and his lighter, but it took her three tries before her trembling fingers would manage the simple action. She handed him the cigarette and then the lighter, her eyes lingering on his hard mouth.

"You've thought about sleeping with me, haven't you?" he asked unexpectedly.

Why lie? she asked herself. She sighed. "Yes."

"There's no reason to be embarrassed. It's a perfectly natural curiosity between two people who've known each other as long as we have." He took a draw from the cigarette. "But you don't want sex outside marriage."

She stared out the windshield. "No," she said honestly.

He glanced at her and then nodded absently. "Okay."

She felt as if she were struggling out of a web of vagueness. Nothing made sense anymore, least of all Ethan's suddenly changed attitude toward her. He wanted her, that was patently obvious. But wasn't it because he couldn't have Miriam? Or was there some reason that she'd missed entirely?

Well, there was going to be plenty of time to figure it out, she supposed. Ethan sat beside her, quietly smoking his cigarette while she shot covert glances his way and tried to understand what he wanted from her. Life was suddenly growing very complicated.

Supper that night was a stilted affair, with Miriam complaining delicately about every dish and eating hardly anything. She glared at Arabella as if she wished her on Mars. Probably, Arabella mused, because she'd seen the two of them when they came in from their ride in the truck. Arabella's hair had been mussed, her makeup missing, her lips obviously swollen. It didn't take a mind reader to know that she and Ethan had been making love.

And in that supposition, Arabella was right. Miriam did recognize the signs and they made her furious. The way Ethan was looking at the younger woman under his thick dark eyelashes was painful to her. Ethan had looked at her that way once, in the early days of their courtship. But now he had eyes only for Arabella, and Miriam's hope for a reconciliation was going up in smoke. Not that she loved Ethan; she didn't. But it hurt her pride that he could love someone else, especially when that someone was Arabella. It had been because of Arabella that Ethan had never fallen completely under Miriam's spell. He'd wanted her, but his heart had always belonged to that young woman sitting beside him. Arabella would have known that, of course, even in the old days. That was why Miriam had fought the divorce. She'd known that Arabella and Ethan would wind up together, and she hadn't wanted it to happen. But all her efforts hadn't stopped it.

Ethan didn't see Miriam's pointed glare. He was too busy watching the expression on Arabella's face. Her mouth had a soft swell where his had pressed against it, and it made him burn with pride to know how easily she'd given in to him at the last. He was a man again, a whole, capable man again, and for the first time, Miriam's presence didn't unsettle him. She'd wounded his ego to the quick with her taunts and ridicule about his prowess in the bedroom. But now he was beginning to understand that it wasn't strictly a physical problem. Not the way his body had reacted to Arabella earlier.

Miriam saw his smug expression and shifted uncomfortably.

"Thinking long thoughts, darling?" she taunted with a cold smile. "Or are you just reminiscing about the way we used to be together?"

Ethan pursed his thin lips and studied her. The anguish he felt from her taunts was suddenly gone. He knew now that the only failure was hers. She was conceited and cold and cruel, a sexless woman who basically hated men and used her beauty to punish them.

"I was thinking that you must have had a hell of a childhood," he replied.

Miriam went stark white. She dropped her fork and fumbled to pick it up again. "What in the world made you say such a thing?" she faltered.

He went from contempt to pity in seconds. Everything suddenly became crystal clear, and he understood her better now than he ever had before. Not that it changed his feelings. He couldn't want her, or love her. But he hated her less.

"No reason," he replied, but not unkindly. "Eat your beef. To hell with what they say about it, red meat's been sustaining human beings for hundreds of years in this country."

"I do seem to have a rather large appetite these days,"

Miriam replied. She glanced at Ethan suspiciously and then dropped her eyes.

Arabella had been watching the byplay with cold misery. Ethan was warming to the older woman, she could feel it. So what did she do now? Should she play up to him or not? She only wanted him to be happy. If that meant helping him get Miriam back, then she supposed she could be strong enough to do it.

As if he sensed her regard, he turned his head and smiled at her. He laid his hand on the table, inviting hers. After a second's hesitation, she slid her fingers across the palm and had them warmly, softly enfolded. He brought them to his mouth and kissed them hungrily, oblivious to his mother's shocked delight and Miriam's bridled anger.

Arabella colored and caught her breath. There had been a breathless tenderness in that caress, and the way he was looking at her made her body ripple with the memory of that afternoon.

"Are we really going to sit through a nature special?" Miriam asked, breaking into the tense silence.

Ethan lifted an eyebrow at her. "Why not? I like polar bears."

"Well, I don't," Miriam muttered. "I hate polar bears, in fact. I hate living out in the country, I hate the sound of animals in the distance, I hate this house, and I even hate you!"

"I thought you wanted to talk about a reconciliation," Ethan pointed out.

"How can I, when you've obviously been out in the fields making love with Miss Concert Pianist!"

Arabella flushed, but Ethan just laughed. The sound was unfamiliar, especially to Miriam.

"As it happens, it was in the truck, not in the fields," Ethan said with outrageous honesty. "And engaged people do make love."

"Yes, I remember," Miriam said icily. She threw her napkin down and stood up. "I think I'll lie down. I'll see you all in the morning. Good night."

She left, and Coreen sat back with a loud sigh. "Thank God! Now I can enjoy what's left of my meal." She picked up a homemade roll and buttered it. "What's this about making love in the pickup?" she asked Ethan with a grin.

"We need to keep Miriam guessing," he replied. He leaned back in his chair and watched his mother. "You tell me what we were doing."

"Arabella's a virgin," Coreen pointed out, noting Arabella's discomfort.

"I know that," Ethan said gently and smiled in her direction. "That won't change. Not even to run Miriam off."

"I didn't think it would." Coreen patted Arabella's hand. "Don't look so embarrassed, dear. Sex is part of life. But you aren't the kind of woman Miriam is. Your conscience would beat you to death. And to be perfectly blunt, so would Ethan's. He's a puritan."

"I'm not alone," Ethan said imperturbably. "What would you call a twenty-two-year-old virgin?"

"Sensible," Coreen replied. "It's dangerous to play around these days, and it's stupid to give a man the benefits of marriage without making him assume responsibility for his pleasure. That isn't just old-fashioned morality, it's common sense. I'm a dyed-in-the-wool women's libber, but I'll be damned if I'd give my body to any man without love and commitment."

Ethan stood up calmly, and pushed his chair toward his mother. "Stand on that," he invited. "If you're going to give a sermon, you need to be seen as well as heard, shrimp."

Coreen drew back the hand holding the roll and Ethan chuckled. He bent and picked his little mother up in his arms and kissed her resoundingly on the cheek.

"I love you," he said as he put her down again, flustered and breathless. "Don't ever change."

"Ethan, you just exasperate me," she muttered.

He kissed her forehead. "That's mutual." He glanced at Arabella, whose eyes were adoring him. "I have to make some phone calls. If she comes back downstairs, come into the office and we'll give her something else to fuss about."

Arabella colored again, but she smiled at him. "All right."

He winked and left the two women at the table.

"You still love him, don't you?" Coreen asked as she sipped her coffee.

Arabella shrugged. "It seems to be an illness without a cure," she agreed. "Despite Miriam and the arguments and all the years apart, I've never wanted anyone else."

"It seems to be mutual."

"Seems to be, yes, but that's just the game we're playing to keep Miriam from getting to him again."

"Isn't it odd how he's changed in one day," Coreen said suddenly, watching the younger woman with narrowed eyes. "This morning he was all starch and bristle when Miriam came, and now he's so relaxed and careless of her pointed remarks that he seems like another man." She narrowed one eye. "Just what did you do to him while the two of you were out alone?"

"I just kissed him, honest," Arabella replied. "But he is different, isn't he?" She frowned. "He said something odd, about being whole again. And he did say that Miriam told him he couldn't satisfy her. Maybe he just needed an ego boost."

His mother smiled secretively and stared down into her coffee. "Maybe he did." She leaned back. "She'll make another play for him, you know. Probably tonight."

"I told him I thought she would, too," Arabella said. "But I couldn't get up enough nerve to offer to sleep with him." She cleared her throat. "He really is a puritan. I thought he'd be outraged if I mentioned it. I could sleep on a chair or something. I didn't mean..." she added, horrified at what his mother might think.

"I know, dear. You don't have to worry about that. But I do think it might be a good idea if you spend some time in his room tonight. Miriam would think twice before she invaded his bedroom if she thought you were in it with him." She grinned. "It would damage her pride."

"Ethan may damage my ears," Arabella said ruefully. "He won't like it. And what if Miriam tells you about it? You're a puritan, too, about having unmarried people sleeping together under your roof."

"I'll pretend to be horrified and surprised and I'll insist that Ethan set a wedding date," Coreen promised.

"Oh, no, you can't!" Arabella gasped.

Coreen got up and began removing crockery. She darted an amused glance at her houseguest. "Don't worry about a thing. I know something you don't. Help me get these things into the kitchen, would you, dear? Betty Ann went home an hour ago, so you can help me do dishes. Then, you can start making plans for later. Do you have a slinky negligee?''

The whole thing was taking on the dimensions of a dream, Arabella thought as she waited in Ethan's room dressed in the risqué white negligee and peignoir that Coreen had given her. How was she ever going to tell him that this was his mother's idea?

She'd brushed her long hair until it shone. She was still wearing her bra under the low-cut gown because she couldn't unfasten the catch and Coreen had already gone to bed. But it did make her breasts look sexier, and the way the satin clung to her body she felt like a femme fatale.

She draped herself across the foot of Ethan's antique four-poster bed, the white satin contrasting violently with the brown-and-black-and white plaid of his coverlet. The room was so starkly masculine that she felt a little out of place in it.

There were a couple of heavy leather armchairs by the fireplace, and a few Indian rugs on the floor. The beige draperies at the windows were old and heavy, blocking out the crescent moon and the expanse of open land. The ceiling light fixture was bold and masculine, shaped like a wagon wheel. There was a tallboy against one wall and a dresser and mirror against another, next to the remodeled walk-in closet. It was a big room, but it suited Ethan. He liked a lot of space.

The door began to open and she struck a pose. Perhaps this was Miriam getting a peek in. She tugged the gown off one shoulder, hating the ugly cast that ruined the whole effect. She put it behind her and pushed her breasts forward, staring toward the door with what she hoped was a seductive smile.

But it wasn't Miriam. It was Ethan, and he stopped dead in the doorway, his fingers in the act of unbuttoning his shirt frozen in place.

Chapter Seven

"Oh!" Arabella gasped. She scrambled into a sitting position, painfully aware of how much cleavage she was showing, not to mention the liquid way the satin adhered to her slender curves.

Ethan slammed the door behind him, his face unreadable. He was bareheaded and he looked very tired and worn, but the light in his eyes was fascinating. He stared at her as if he'd never seen a woman's body before, lingering on the thrust of her breasts under the satin with its exquisite, lacy trim.

"My God," he breathed finally. "You could bring a man to his knees."

It wasn't what she'd expected him to say, but it made her efforts with her appearance worthwhile. "I could?" she echoed blankly as delight made her face radiant.

He moved toward her. His shirt was halfway unbuttoned, and he looked rough and dangerous and very sexy with his hair disheveled and that faint growth of beard on his deeply tanned face.

"Is the bra really necessary, or couldn't you get it off?" he asked as he sat down beside her on the coverlet.

She smiled shyly. "I couldn't get it off," she admitted, lifting the cast. "I still can't use these fingers."

He smiled gently. "Come here." He tugged her forward and reached around her, his lean, rough-skinned hands pushing the straps down over her arms to give him access to the fastening. But the bodice was loose and it fell to her waist, giving him a total view of her breasts in their brief, lacy covering.

He caught his breath. His body made a quick, emphatic statement about what her curves did to it and he laughed even through the discomfort. "My God," he said, chuckling deeply.

"What is it?" she asked breathlessly.

"Don't ask." He reached behind her and unfastened the bra, amused at her efforts to catch the front as it fell. She held it against her, but one of his hands went to her smooth, bare back and began to caress it gently.

"Let it fall," he whispered against her lips as he took them.

It was the most erotic experience of her life, even more than the interlude by the swimming hole, because she was a woman now and her love for him had grown. She released the fabric and her good arm went up around his neck, lifting her breasts.

He drew back to look down at them with pure male appreciation. His fingers touched her, and he looked into her eyes, watching the pupils dilate as he teased the soft contour of her breast and brushed his forefinger tenderly over the taut nipple. She bit back a moan and his free hand lanced into the thick hair at her nape and contracted. He held her prisoner with delicious sensuality while his other hand snaked to her waist and around her, lifting her body in a delicate arch.

"I've dreamed of this," he said, lowering his eyes and then his hard, warm mouth to the swollen softness of her breast.

She watched his mouth open as it settled on her, felt the soft, warm suction, felt the rough drag of his tongue, the faint threat of his teeth and a sound she'd never made pushed out of her throat.

He heard it. His arousal grew by the second, until he was shaking with the force of it. She was everything he'd ever wanted. Young, virginal, achingly receptive to his advances, glorying in his need of her, giving of herself without reservation. He could barely believe what was happening.

His dark eyebrows drew together in harsh pleasure as he increased the pressure of his mouth, feeling her shiver as the intensity of the caress grew. He felt her nails digging into his back and he groaned, his lean hand sweeping down her waist to her hip, edging the fabric up until he could touch her soft, bare thigh.

"Ethan, no…!" she whispered frantically, but his head lifted from her breast and he eased her back onto the coverlet, knowing she was helpless now, totally at his mercy in a sensual limbo.

"I'm not going to hurt you," he said gently, bending over her. "Unbutton my shirt." His fingers slid between her legs, tenderly separating them, and he watched her face waver between acceptance and fear of the unknown. He bent to her lips, brushing them with soft reassurance.

"I want to make love to you," he whispered. "We don't have to go all the way."

"I don't understand," she choked.

He kissed her accusing eyes shut. "I'll teach you. One way or another, I'm going to be your lover. It might as well begin now. Get my shirt out of the way, sweet," he breathed into her open mouth. "And then lift your body against mine and let me feel your breasts against my skin."

She'd never dreamed that men said things like that to women, but it had an incredible effect on her emotions. She cried out, her hands fumbling buttons out of buttonholes, and then she arched up, pulling him down on her with the one good arm she had. The experience was staggering. She shuddered as his hair-roughened skin dragged against hers in a terribly arousing caress, weeping helplessly in his arms.

He groaned. All his dreams were coming true. This was his Arabella, and she wanted him. She wanted him!

He eased one powerful leg between hers, and he caught her hand without lifting his mouth and pulled it up against his taut stomach.

"I can't!" she protested wildly.

"You can, sweetheart," he said against her mouth. "Touch me like this," he whispered, opening her clenched fingers and splaying them against his body. "Arabella. Arabella, I need you so!" he ground out. His fingers trembled as they guided hers. "Don't stop," he groaned harshly, dragging in an audible breath as his teeth clenched.

She watched his face with astonished awe. He let her watch, glorying in the forbidden pleasure of her touch, aching to tell her how incredible this was for him, but he couldn't get words out.

The sudden opening of the door was a cruel, vicious shock.

"Oh, for God's sake!" Miriam exclaimed, horrified. She went out again, slamming the door, her furious voice echoing down the hall along with her running feet.

Ethan shuddered helplessly above Arabella. He rolled over onto his back, groaning.

She sat up, her breasts still bare, her eyes apprehensive. "Are you all right?" she asked hesitantly.

"Not really," he managed with a rueful smile. He laughed in spite of the throbbing ache in his body. "But, oh, God, what a beautiful ache it is, little one."

She tugged the gown up over her breasts, frowning slightly. "I don't understand, Ethan," she said.

He laughed, keeping his secret to himself. "It's just as well that you don't. Not yet, anyway." He lay breathing deeply until he could control it, until the ache began to subside, and all the while his silver eyes lanced over her face and her body with tender delight.

"Miriam saw us," she said uncomfortably.

"Wasn't that the whole idea?" he asked.

"Well, yes. But…" She colored and averted her eyes.

He sat up, stretching lazily before he brought her face up to his and began to press soft, undemanding kisses over it. "Women have been touching men like that since the beginning of time," he whispered at her closed eyelids. "I'll bet most of your girlfriends at school indulged, including Mary."

"But she wouldn't…!"

"If she was in love, why not?" He lifted his head and searched her worried face. "Arabella, it's not a sin to want someone. Especially not when you care deeply for them. It's a physical expression of something intangible."

"I have a lot of hang-ups..." she began.

He brushed back her damp, disheveled hair. "You have principles. I can understand that. I'm not going to seduce you in my own bed, in case you were wondering." His pale eyes twinkled with humor. He felt alive as never before, masculine, capable of anything. He brushed his mouth lazily over her nose. "We'll save sex for our wedding night."

She stared at him. "I beg your pardon?"

"Marriage is inevitable," he said. "Miriam isn't going to go away, not if you spend every night in here to keep her out. She's the kind of woman who doesn't understand rejection. She's got her mind made up that she's back to stay, and she thinks she can bulldoze me into it."

"She should know better."

"Oh, but she thinks she has an edge," he murmured. He looked down at her hand, clutching the gown to her body. "Let go of that," he murmured. "I love looking at you."

"Ethan!"

He chuckled. "You love letting me, so you can stop pretending. I've spent a lot of years being convinced that I wasn't a man anymore, so you'll have to forgive me for sounding a little arrogant right now. I've just learned something shocking about myself."

"What?" she asked breathlessly.

"That I'm not impotent," he said simply.

She frowned. Didn't that mean that a man couldn't...?

Her eyes widened. "That was what Miriam meant when she taunted you!"

"You've got it," he agreed. "She couldn't arouse me with all her tricks. It was why I was able to get her to leave. But she wouldn't give me a divorce. She was sure she could get me back under her spell. What she didn't realize was that I was never really under it in the first place. I was briefly infatuated in a purely physical sense. But a craving, once indulged, is usually satisfied. Mine was."

"I guessed she'd know what to do in bed," she sighed. "I'm such a coward…."

He drew her face into his warm, damp throat and smoothed her dark hair gently. "Intimacy is hard, even for men, the first time, Arabella," he said at her ear. "You'll get used to it. I'll never hurt you."

"I know that." And she did. But would he ever be able to love her? That was what she wanted most in the world. She clung to him with a long sigh. "You really don't feel that with Miriam?" she asked lazily. "She's so beautiful and experienced."

His hands hardened on her bare back. "She isn't a patch on you," he said huskily. "She never was."

But you married her, she wanted to say. You loved her, and tonight at supper, you were so gentle with her. But she never got the words out. His hands had tugged the fabric away from her breasts while she was busy thinking, and he wrapped her up against his bare chest with slow expertise, his fingers warm on her rib cage as he traced it.

She moaned and he smiled against her forehead.

"I'd had women by the time you were eighteen," he whispered. "But I felt more with you that day by the swimming hole than I'd ever felt with any of the others, and we did less than I'd ever done with a woman. I've dreamed about that day ever since."

"But you married Miriam," she said quietly. She closed her eyes, unaware of Ethan's expression. "And that says it all, doesn't it? You never loved me. You just wanted me. That's all it's ever going to be. Oh, let me go, Ethan!" She wept, pushing at his shoulders.

But he tightened his hold, easing her down on the bed with him. "It isn't just wanting," he said gently. "Don't fight me," he breathed, settling his mouth on hers. "Don't fight me, honey."

Tears rolled down her face into his hard mouth, but he didn't stop until she was pliant and moaning under the crush of his long, powerful body. Only then did he lift his head and look down at her soft, enraptured face.

His silver eyes searched hers. "If desire was all I felt, do you think I'd spare your chastity?"

She swallowed. "I don't guess you would."

"A man in the throes of passion doesn't usually give a damn what he says or does to get a woman's cooperation," he replied. "I could have had you this afternoon. I could have had you just now. But I stopped."

That could also mean that he didn't want her enough to press his advantage, but she didn't say it.

He sat up, his eyes skimming with warm appreciation over her breasts before he covered them himself, pulling the straps of her gown back up her arms. "You don't have much self-confidence, do you?" he asked when she was standing again. He got to his own feet, towering over her, deliciously sensuous with his chest bare and his mouth faintly swollen from her kisses. "I'll have to work on that."

"It's just to keep Miriam at bay, or so you said," she reminded him shakily.

"Yes, I did say that." He ran his forefinger down her nose. "But in order to do this properly, you're going to have to marry me." He grinned. "It won't be that bad. You can sleep with me and we'll make babies. We'll have a good life together, even if that hand won't let you do anything except give piano lessons."

"And you think that would be enough to satisfy me?" she asked sadly.

The smile left his face. He thought she loved him. She'd acted as if she had. Was she telling him that marriage wouldn't be enough, that she wanted her career instead? He scowled.

"Don't you think you could be happy here?" he asked.

She shifted restlessly. "I'm tired, Ethan. I don't want to talk about marriage tonight. All right?"

He drew a cigarette from his pocket and lit it, still frowning down at her. "All right. But sooner or later you and I are going to have a showdown."

"Meanwhile, I'll do everything I can to help you send Miriam off. If you're sure you want to," she added hesitantly.

"You can't think I want her back?" he demanded.

"Can't you?" she asked sadly, her heart in her soft green eyes.

"Didn't you hear what I told you earlier? Do you know what impotent means?" he added angrily, and gave her the slang for it, watching her face color.

"I—I—know what it means!" she stammered. She moved away from him. "I don't know that I like being a catalyst in that way. Maybe you really want Miriam but you're too afraid of losing her again to…to be capable with her. She betrayed you once…."

"Oh, hell." He took a draw from his cigarette and sighed angrily. He couldn't get through to her what he felt, and he was too tired to try tonight, anyway. There was time. He hoped there was enough. "You'd better get back to your own room before Miriam drags my mother up here and gives her the shock of her life."

"She wouldn't be shocked," she said absently.

"What makes you think so?"

She lifted her eyes. "Because this was her idea. She even gave me the negligee."

"My God! Women!" he burst out.

"We were saving you from Miriam."

"Fair enough. Who's going to save you from me?" he asked, his hands catching her waist and holding fast as he bent toward her mouth. "I want you. Take off your gown and get into bed. I'll love you up to the ceiling."

She tingled all over. "It isn't me you want, it's Miriam!" she sputtered, pulling away from him.

"You blind little bat," he said, shaking his head. "All right, run. But I'll be two steps behind you from now on. I let you get away once. Never again."

She didn't understand that, either. He was saying a lot of strange things. She colored, wondering at his response to her when he said it didn't happen with Miriam. But she was still certain that it had some psychological basis, that inability, and probably it had been triggered by the fear that Miriam would take his heart and betray him again. She didn't want to think about it. It hurt too much. Ethan's ardor had uplifted and upset her, all at once. She'd have the memory of it, but it would be a bittersweet one. She'd always feel that she was nothing more than a physical substitute for the woman he loved.

"I'll lead my own life, thank you," she said, moving toward the door. "I haven't forgotten what you said to me when you told me not to come back to the ranch all those years ago, Ethan."

"You will," he replied, opening the door for her. "You don't know why I said it."

She looked up at him. "But I do. You wanted me out of the way."

"So that I could marry Miriam," he suggested.

"Yes."

He sighed, letting the cigarette dangle in his hand while he searched Arabella's soft eyes. "There are none so blind as those who will not see," he murmured. "You were eighteen," he said quietly. "You were your father's emotional slave, a talented novice with an incredible career potential and infatuated for the first time in your innocent life. You're almost the age I was then. Think about how it would be for you, if our positions were reversed. Think about what you'd feel, and what you'd think, and what you might do about it."

She stared up at him helplessly. "What did my age have to do with it?" she faltered.

"Everything." His face hardened. "My God, don't you see? Arabella, what if I'd made you pregnant that day by the swimming hole?"

Her face went white. She could imagine the horror her father would have felt. She knew what he'd have done, too. She'd never have been allowed to have a child out of wedlock. Ethan might have insisted on marrying her, if he'd known, but he'd have been forced into it.

"I might not have gotten pregnant," she said hesitantly. "Some women never do."

"A few can't, that's so," he replied. "But the majority of women can and do. I wasn't prepared that day, and I can't for one minute imagine holding back long enough to protect you. There's every chance that we'd have created a child together." His eyes grew darker, warmer. "I'd like that," he said huskily. "Oh, God, I'd like making you pregnant, Arabella."

She felt hot all over. She managed to get her fingers on the doorknob. "I'd better...go to bed, Ethan," she managed unsteadily.

"You'd like it, too, wouldn't you?" he asked knowingly, smiling in a way that made her toes curl.

"We aren't married," she said, trying to hold on to her sanity.

"We will be." He leaned against the door facing her, his eyes possessive on her satin-and-lace-clad body. "I won't mind changing diapers and giving bottles, just for the record. I'm not one of those Neanderthal men who think anything short of football and beer is woman's work."

She stared up at him with a soft glow in her face, giving in despite her misgivings. "What if I couldn't give you a baby?" she whispered softly.

He smiled tenderly and touched her mouth with his fingertips. "Then you and I would become closer than most couples do, I suppose," he said, his voice deep and gentle. "We'd be inseparable. We could adopt a child, or maybe several of them, or we could do volunteer work that involved children." He bent and kissed her eyes closed. "Don't ever think that you're only of value to me because of your potential as a mother. Children are, and should be, a precious fringe benefit of marriage. They shouldn't be the only reason for it."

She'd never dreamed of hearing Ethan say such a thing to her. Tears ran down her cheeks and she began to sob.

"Oh, for God's sake…!" He bent and picked her up in his arms, shaken by her reaction. "Arabella, don't," he whispered. His mouth covered hers, faintly tremulous as he savored the tear-wet softness of it, the kiss absolutely beyond his experience as he held her, rocking her in his arms. His head began to spin. Her good arm was around his neck, and she was kissing him back, moaning softly under the crush of his lips, trembling in his protective embrace.

"Now, now, I'm all for the spirit of the thing, but let's not carry it to extremes," Coreen Hardeman murmured dryly.

Ethan lifted his head and stared blankly at his mother. She was leaning against the wall, her gray eyes so smugly pleased that Ethan actually flushed.

Chapter Eight

Arabella was much more embarrassed than Ethan or his indomitable parent. She colored delicately and stiffened in Ethan's arms.

"Uh, shouldn't you put me down?" Arabella asked.

"Why?" Ethan murmured dryly. "It was just getting to the good part."

"I thought it already had, from what Miriam said," Coreen replied, and then spoiled her disapproving-mother stance by bursting into laughter. "You two are heading straight for a fiery end, or so I'm told. Shameful behavior, and Arabella such an innocent." She raised an eyebrow at Ethan. "How could you, and other platitudes."

Ethan grinned. "I had a lot of cooperation," he returned, with a wicked glance at Arabella.

"Miriam said that, too," Coreen nodded.

"You put me down, you corrupting influence!" Arabella muttered, struggling. "I knew you'd lead me astray if I wasn't careful."

He set her gently on her feet. "Would you like to try again? I seem to remember finding you lying in exquisite repose on my bed…?" He glanced at Coreen. "She said it was your idea, too."

"Actually, it was," Coreen confessed. "I didn't know what else to do. I was absolutely certain that Miriam would make a play for you, and I had a fairly good idea why. I think she's pregnant."

"So Arabella told me." He rubbed a hand over his broad chest, staring appreciatively at the younger of the two women. "We're getting married. Arabella doesn't know it yet, but you might go ahead and start making the arrangements and we'll get her to the altar before she has time to work it out."

"Good idea." Coreen laughed delightedly. "Oh, Arabella, I couldn't be more pleased. You'll be the most wonderful daughter-in-law."

"But…" Arabella began, looking from mother to son with dazed eyes.

"She will at that," Ethan agreed. "I'll take her downtown tomorrow to buy a ring. What do you think about having the wedding at the Methodist church? Reverend Boland could perform the service."

"Yes, he'll do nicely. And we can have the reception at the Jacobsville Inn. It's big enough. I'll ask Shelby Ballenger if she'll help with the arrangements. She did the most beautiful job with our charity fashion show last month—amazing how well she manages her volunteer work and their two sons at the same time."

"Do that," Ethan replied. "Now, how about the invitations?"

"I don't think—" Arabella tried again.

"That's a good idea. Don't," Ethan said approvingly. He folded his arms across his chest and turned back to his mother. "Can you handle the invitations?"

"It's my wedding!" Arabella burst out. "Surely I can do something to help!"

"Of course you can," Ethan agreed. "You can try on the wedding gown. Take her to the best store in Houston," he told his mother, "and find the most expensive gown they have. Don't let her get away with something ordinary."

"I won't," Coreen promised. "A white wedding," she sighed. "I never thought I'd live to see you happily married, Ethan."

He was watching Arabella with an odd kind of tenderness. "Neither did I. Not like this," he said huskily, and his eyes blazed.

But it's only to get Miriam out of his life for good, Arabella wanted to wail. He doesn't love me, he wants me. I make him whole again physically. But that's no reason to get married!

She started to tell him that, but he was already going back into his room.

"I think I'll lock the door, just in case," he chuckled. "Good night, Mother." He stared at Arabella. "Good night, little one."

"Good night, Ethan," Arabella said softly. "But, there's just one thing—"

He closed the door before she could tell him what it was.

"I hate to look smug, but I can't help it," Coreen said with a smile as she walked down the hall with Arabella. "Miriam was so certain she could get under Ethan's skin again. I couldn't bear to see her hurt him so badly twice."

"He was different with her at supper," Arabella said, voicing her biggest fear, that Ethan was once again falling under his ex-wife's spell.

Coreen glanced at her. "Ethan is deep. Don't worry. He wouldn't marry you just to chase Miriam away. I can guarantee it," she added, looking as if she wanted to say something more. But she shrugged and smiled faintly. "I'd better get to bed. Sleep tight, darling, and congratulations."

"Nothing happened," Arabella blurted out. "I don't know what Miriam said—"

Coreen patted her cheek gently. "I know you, and I know my son. You don't have to tell me anything. Besides," she added with a grin, "men who aren't frustrated don't look like Ethan looked when he went back into his room. I'm old, but I'm not blind. 'Night!"

Arabella stared after her, nervous and uncertain. She went on down the hall, hoping against hope that she wouldn't encounter Miriam on the way to her room.

She should have known the woman would be lying in wait for her. Miriam opened her door just as Arabella drew even with it. Her face was flushed and her eyes were red. She'd obviously been crying.

"You snake," Miriam accused furiously. She threw

back her auburn hair contemptuously. "He's mine! I'm not going to give him up without a fight!"

"Then you can have one," Arabella said quietly. "We're getting married. Ethan told you so."

"He won't marry you," the other woman replied. "He loves me! He always has! He only wants you." She let her eyes punctuate that coldly sarcastic remark. "You're quite a novelty, but you'll wear thin pretty quickly. You'll never get him to the altar."

"He's making the wedding arrangements already."

"He won't marry you, I tell you!" Miriam flashed. "He only divorced me because I ran around on him."

"That seems like a good reason to me," Arabella returned. She was shaking inside, but she wouldn't back down. "You hurt his pride."

"What do you think it did to mine, having you thrown in my face from the day we married?" she burst out. "It was always Arabella this, Arabella that, from the whole damned family! Nobody could have lived up to you, nobody! I hated you from the start, because Ethan wanted you!" Her eyes were wet with tears and she was sobbing as she tried to speak. "Imagine that!" she laughed brokenly. "I had twice your experience and sophistication, I was more beautiful and sought-after than you could ever hope to be. But it was you he wanted, your name he whispered when he made love to me." She leaned against the wall, crying helplessly while Arabella gaped at her.

"Wha...what?" Arabella gasped.

"It was only when I accused him of using me as a substitute for you that he stopped being capable of making love to me," Miriam said, slumping. "He was obsessed with your body. He still is. Probably," she added, rallying a little, "because he's never had it. Now he'll get his fill of you, and then maybe I can have him back. Maybe I can make him want me. He did love me," she whispered achingly. "He loved me, but I couldn't make him want me, too. Damn you, Arabella! He would have wanted me if it hadn't been for you!'"

She went back into her room and slammed the door, leaving a shocked, staggered Arabella in the hall.

She managed to get into her room without really seeing where she was going. She fumbled the light switch on and locked the door before she collapsed on the bed.

Was Miriam telling the truth? Had Ethan been so obsessed by her body that it even affected his marriage? Was it possible for a man to love one woman but lust after another? She knew so little, had such a faint experience of men that she didn't know.

The one thing she was certain of was that Ethan still wanted her. It might not be enough to base a marriage on, but she loved him more than her own life. If desire was all he had to give her, perhaps she could build on that and teach him, someday, to love her. She wasn't as beautiful as Miriam, but he'd said once that inner qualities were just as important.

His ardor that afternoon and that night were proof that his so-called impotence with Miriam was just a fluke. Surely if he could want one woman, he could want another? Miriam had hurt his pride and his body had rebelled. But at supper he'd warmed to Miriam, so might that not affect his ability to want the other woman? Miriam had declared war in the hall and Arabella was afraid that she might not be able to compete. Especially when compared to the more beautiful older woman.

Her mind gave her no peace at all. It was much later when she closed her eyes and went to sleep, leaving all the worries behind.

Things looked a little brighter when she awoke the next morning. She had to be more confident. She could work at her appearance, at her personality. Perhaps she could become like Miriam, and then Ethan might be able to love her. She might still get Miriam to acknowledge defeat, using her own tactics against her.

She put on her prettiest pale green cotton sundress with its dropped square neck and cinched waist and full skirt. It was a flirty kind of dress and it matched her eyes. She put her hair into a neatly coiled chignon on top of her head and deliberately used more makeup than normal. She had a pair of huge earrings she'd never liked, but she wore those, too. The result was a much more sophisticated version of herself. She smiled seductively and nodded. Yes. If a sophisticated woman was what Ethan wanted, she could be that. Certainly she could!

She went downstairs with a bounce in her stride. If only it wasn't for the stupid cast, she might really look seductive, she thought, glaring at the bulky thing. Well, only a little while longer and it would be off, then she could really do some important shopping for the right clothes.

When she got to the breakfast table, Ethan and Miriam were already there, with Coreen and the housekeeper, Betty Ann, busy alternating between kitchen and dining room with platters of food.

Miriam and Ethan appeared to be in intense conversation, and not a hostile one, because he was smiling gently and Miriam was hanging on his every word. Miriam even looked different this morning. Her long hair was plaited and hanging down her back. She was wearing a T-shirt and jeans and no makeup at all. What a change, Arabella thought almost hysterically. She and the other woman looked their own opposites.

Ethan turned and saw Arabella and his jaw clenched. His eyes narrowed with something she couldn't quite define.

"Well, good morning," she called gaily, bluffing it out. She bent over Ethan's tall figure and brushed her mouth teasingly over his nose. "How are you? And how are you, Miriam? Isn't it a beautiful morning?"

Miriam murmured something appropriate and concentrated on her coffee, giving Arabella a glare before she lifted her cup to her lips.

Arabella sat down, still with a bounce, and poured herself a cup of coffee. "I guess Coreen and I will go to Houston today to find my wedding gown, if you don't mind, Ethan," she said breezily. "I do want something exquisite."

Ethan stared down into his coffee cup. Images of the past were dancing before his eyes. Miriam had said something similar when they became engaged. She'd even looked as Arabella did now, oh, so sophisticated and lighthearted. Had he been completely and totally wrong about Arabella? Did money matter to her now that she was apparently without a career, now that she couldn't earn her own way? Or was she trying to compete with Miriam by becoming the same kind of woman? Mentally he dismissed the latter. Arabella knew he didn't want another Miriam. She wouldn't make the mistake of trying to emulate a woman he despised. He couldn't bear the thought of another marriage like his first one. Why had he committed himself? He'd wanted to get rid of Miriam, but now it seemed he might be walking back into the same trap.

Coreen came in with a plate of biscuits, took a look at Arabella and did a double take. "Arabella? How… different you look, dear."

"Do you like it?" Arabella asked with a smile. "I thought I'd try something new. Do you feel like going to Houston with me today?"

Coreen put the plate of biscuits down. "Certainly. If you'd like to.…"

"By all means, go ahead," Miriam said huskily. "I'll keep Ethan company," she added with a rather shy smile at her ex-husband.

Ethan didn't answer. He was still trying to absorb the change in Arabella.

He didn't say anything to her all through breakfast and Arabella began to feel nervous. He and Miriam had been talking earnestly, and now he looked uncomfortable when she'd mentioned the wedding gown. Was he having second thoughts? Didn't he want to marry her after all?

Suddenly, he got up from the table and started out of the room.

"Just a minute, Ethan," Miriam called quickly, seeing her chance. "I need to ask you something."

She ran to join him, clutching seductively at his arm as they went outside together.

"What a nice way to start the morning," Arabella said over her second cup of coffee about half an hour later.

Coreen patted her hand. "Don't worry so. Let's get

going. I'll just run into the kitchen and tell Betty Ann where we'll be."

While Arabella continued to think about the scene at breakfast, the phone rang and she got up to answer it, since Coreen and Betty Ann were occupied.

Considering the sour note the day had started on, she should have expected it to be her father, she thought when his curt voice came over the line.

"How are you?" he asked stiffly.

She curled the cord around her fingers. "I'm much better, thank you," she replied, her tone just as stilted.

"And your hand?"

"I won't know until the cast comes off," she said.

"I hope you had the sense to let an orthopedic surgeon look at it," he said after a minute.

"A specialist was called in, yes," she replied. Her father made her feel ten years old again. "There's a good chance that I may be able to play normally again."

"Your host filed an injunction against me, so that I can't touch the joint account," he told her. "That wasn't kind of you, Arabella. I have to live, too."

She bit her lip. "I...I know, but..."

"You'll have to send me a check," he continued. "I can't live off my brother. I'll need at least five hundred to get me through. Thank God we had good insurance. And I'll want to hear from you as soon as your cast is off and you've seen the specialist."

She hesitated. She wanted to tell him that she was marrying Ethan, but she couldn't get the words out. It was amazing how he intimidated her, and she a grown woman! It was habit, she supposed. He'd always controlled her. He still did. She was just a wimp, she thought angrily.

"I'll…call you," she promised.

"Don't forget the check. You know Frank's address."

That was all. No words of affection, no comfort. He hung up. She stood staring blankly at the receiver. Before she had time to show her concern, Coreen was back and they were off to Houston in Coreen's black Mercedes-Benz.

They browsed through the exclusive bridal department at an exclusive store in Houston for an hour before Arabella was able to choose between three exquisite designer gowns. The one she settled on was traditional with Alençon lace over white *peau de soie*, a delicate, modified V neckline that plunged to the waist but in such a way as to be discreet. It was unique and incredibly sensuous all at once. She chose a traditional veil as well, one with yards and yards of fabric which Ethan would be required to lift during the ceremony. Arabella felt the sense of tradition to her toes, because she was going to her wedding bed a virgin.

The pleasure of the day had been faintly spoiled by Ethan's attitude and Miriam's changed image. Arabella still didn't understand what had gone wrong so suddenly, and even as she was choosing the gown she wondered if she'd really get to wear it. Ethan could change his mind. She wouldn't even blame him. Probably he was finding it hard going to give up Miriam, and the divorce had only been final for three months. Coreen had said that he'd been moody during those three months, too. She frowned at the gown as the saleswoman wrapped it with care in its distinctive box.

"What a blessing you're a perfect size," Coreen smiled. "No alterations. That's a good omen."

Arabella managed a wan smile. "I could use one."

The older woman gave her a curious look as she gave the saleswoman her credit card. But it wasn't until they'd completed their shopping, right down to delicate silk-and-lace undergarments and nylon hose, and were on their way back to Jacobsville that she finally asked Arabella what was wrong.

"I wish I knew why Ethan was so distant this morning," she told the other woman.

"Miriam's doing, no doubt," Coreen said curtly. "Don't underestimate her. Ethan's treating her too nicely and she likes it."

"I won't underestimate her." She hesitated. "That phone call I got this morning was from my father. He called and asked me to send him a check…." She cleared her throat. "Well, he's still my father," she said defensively.

"Of course he is."

"I should have paid for the gown," she said suddenly. "Then, if the wedding is called off, it won't put any strain on your budget."

"Listen, dear, our budget doesn't get strained and you know it." She frowned at Arabella. "This was Ethan's idea. He wanted you to have a designer gown."

"I think he's changed his mind. He and Miriam were getting thick before breakfast," Arabella said miserably.

Coreen sighed gently. "Oh, Arabella, I wish I knew what was in my eldest's mind. Surely he isn't letting that woman get under his skin again!"

"Miriam said that he wanted me when he married her," Arabella blurted out. Her lower lip trembled. "She accused me of ruining her marriage."

"Ethan's always wanted you," the older woman said surprisingly. "He should have married you instead of letting your father spirit you away. He was never happy with Miriam. I've always felt that she was just a stopgap for him, a poor substitute for you. Perhaps Miriam realized it, and that was what went wrong."

"Wanting isn't loving." Arabella twisted her purse in her lap. "I may not be sophisticated, but I know that."

"You look pretty uptown to me today," Coreen comforted with a smile. "That sundress is very attractive, and I like the way you're wearing your hair. Ethan certainly noticed," she added wickedly.

"I thought Miriam was getting his undivided attention this morning and he wasn't snarling at her."

"Men get funny when they start thinking about marriage," Coreen assured her. "Now, stop worrying. Ethan knows what he's doing."

But did he? Arabella wondered. She might be helping him to make an even bigger mistake than he had before.

And when they got back to the ranch, she found more cause than ever to be concerned. Betty Ann was coming down the staircase with a tray when Coreen and Arabella walked in with the huge dress box.

"What are you doing carrying a tray upstairs at this hour?" Coreen asked the housekeeper, and frowned.

Arabella had a faint premonition even as Betty Ann spoke.

"Ethan fell," Betty Ann said tersely. "Had to be took to the hospital and X-rayed, with herself—" she jerked her head toward the staircase "—hanging on him for dear life."

"Is he all right?" Coreen asked the question for both of them.

"Mild concussion, nothing really serious. They wanted to keep him overnight, but he insisted on coming home." The housekeeper sighed. "He's been up in his room ever since, with herself hovering, and when he wasn't demanding things, he was cussing." She glanced warily at Arabella. "I don't know what Miriam told him, but he's been anxious to see Arabella. Too anxious and too angry."

Arabella felt her knees going weak. Could her father have called back and told Ethan about the check he'd demanded? She knew Ethan would be furious. She just hadn't counted on him finding out so quickly. How had he found out?

"I guess I'd better go up and see him," she murmured.

"We both will," Coreen said shortly.

They marched upstairs. Ethan was lying on top of his bed with a faint gash on his forehead that had been stitched, making a red-and-black pattern on the dark skin. He was fully clothed, and Miriam was sitting with an angelic look by his bedside. The ministering angel.

"So you finally came back," Ethan began, glaring at Arabella. "I hope you enjoyed your shopping trip."

"You knew we were going to get my wedding gown," she said, mildly defensive.

"It's lovely, too, one of their most expensive," Coreen seconded. "A designer gown…"

"Yes, I had one of theirs when I was married," Miriam said with a demure flirting glance at Ethan. "Didn't I, darling?"

"What happened to you?" Coreen asked.

"I got tossed," Ethan said shortly. "Every rider comes off now and again. I was helping Randy with that new mustang in the string we bought from Luke Harper. I got pitched into the fence on my way down. It's nothing."

"Except concussion," Coreen muttered.

"Obviously that didn't bother anybody except Miriam," he said enigmatically, glaring at his mother and Arabella.

Coreen glared back at him. "You're in a sweet mood, I see. Well, I'll help Betty Ann. Are you coming, Miriam?" she added pointedly.

"Oh, no. I'll sit with Ethan. He shouldn't be alone, since he has a concussion," Miriam said, smiling as she laid a protective hand on Ethan's big, lean one.

Coreen went out. Arabella didn't know what to do. Ethan didn't look as if he needed protecting from his ex-wife, and the way he was looking at Arabella made her want to hide.

"Did you hear from my father?" she asked him hesitantly.

"No, I didn't hear from your father," he said coldly. "Get me a beer, will you, Miriam?"

Miriam looked as if leaving was the last thing she wanted to do, but Ethan glared at her and she left, reluctantly, her eyes darting nervously from Ethan to Arabella.

That nervous glance made better sense when she closed the door and Ethan let Arabella have it with both barrels.

"Thank you for your loving concern," he said coldly. "How kind of you to give a damn if I killed myself on a horse!"

She felt her knees going weak. "What do you mean?" she asked.

"You might have told Mother, at least," he persisted. He tried to sit up, grimaced and grabbed his head, but he scowled furiously when she made an automatic move toward him. "Just keep your distance, honey," he said harshly. "I don't want your belated attention. Miriam was here, thank God. She looked after me."

"I don't understand what you're talking about," she said, exasperated.

"You had a phone call before you left the ranch, didn't you?" he demanded.

"Why, yes, of course…" she began.

"Miriam told you I'd been hurt and I needed Mother to drive me in to the hospital, but you didn't say anything," he accused. "Not one word to her. Were you getting even, because I didn't pay you enough attention at breakfast? Or was it a way to get back at me for what happened last night? Did I go too far and scare you out of your virginal wits?"

Her head was swimming. Surely he wasn't quite rational after that knock on the head, with all these wild statements. "Ethan, Miriam didn't call me," she protested. "I didn't know you were hurt!"

"You just admitted that you got the phone call, so don't bother denying it," he added furiously when she started to do just that, to explain that it was her father who called, not Miriam. "I should never have divorced Miriam. When the chips were down, she cared and you didn't. I hope that damned dress you brought is returnable, honey, because I wouldn't marry you on a bet! Now get out of my room!"

"Ethan!" she burst out, horrified that he could actually believe her capable of such hard-boiled behavior.

"I only took you in because I felt sorry for you," he said, giving her a cold appraisal with silver eyes. "I wanted you like hell, but marriage is too high a price to pay for a mercenary virgin with eyes like cash registers. It's all too plain now that I was right, that all you were interested in was financial security for you, and probably for your damned father!" Before she could answer that unfounded charge, he sat straight up in bed, glaring. "I said get out! I don't want to see you again!"

"If you believe I'm that mercenary, then I'll go," she replied, shaking with mingled hurt and fury. "I'm glad to know how you really feel about me, that it was only desire and pity all along."

His eyes flashed silver fire. "The same goes for me. You're no different than Miriam was—out for all you can get. You even look like she used to!"

So that was it. Too late, she realized how her sudden change of appearance and her interest in an expensive wedding gown must have seemed to a man who'd already been used for his wealth once.

"You don't understand," she began.

"Oh, yes, I do," he returned hotly. His head was throbbing. Somewhere inside, he knew he was being unreasonable, but he could hardly think at all for pain and outrage. "Will you get out!"

She went. She could barely see through her tears, almost bumping into a satisfied-looking Miriam as she went down the hall toward her own room. Her temper flared at the smug expression on the older woman's face.

"Congratulations," she flashed at Miriam. "You've

got what you wanted. I hope your conscience lets you enjoy it—if you have one."

Miriam shifted uncomfortably. "I told you he's mine," she said defensively.

"He was never yours," Arabella said, brushing angrily at her tears. "He was never mine, either, but at least I loved him! You only wanted what he had, I heard you say so before you married him. It isn't your heart that he broke, it was your ego. He was the one who got away, and you couldn't take it! So now you're going to get him back, but you'll be cheating him. You don't love him, even now. And if you're not pregnant, I'm a brain surgeon!"

Miriam went white. "What did you say?" she gasped.

"You heard me," Arabella said. "What are you going to do, get Ethan to the altar and pretend it's his? That's just what he needs now, to have you come back and finish what you started. You almost destroyed him once. Are you going to finish the job?"

"I need someone!" Miriam protested.

"Try the father of the child you're carrying," Arabella replied.

Miriam wrapped her arms around her chest. "My child is none of your business. And neither is Ethan. If he loved you, he'd never have believed you could ignore him when he was hurt."

Arabella nodded quietly. "Yes, I know that," she said, pain deepening her tone. "And that's the only reason I'm leaving. If I thought he cared, even a little, I'd stay and fight you to the death. But if it's you he wants, then I can bow out gracefully." She laughed bitterly. "I should be used to it. I did it four years ago, and look how happy you made him."

Miriam grimaced "It could be different this time."

"It could. But it won't. You don't love him," Arabella said. "That's what makes it so terrible, even if he loves you." She turned away and went into her room sickened by the thought. It was like history repeating itself.

The wedding gown, in its box, was lying on her bed. She tossed it into a chair and threw herself across the bed, crying her heart out. It didn't matter that Miriam was the snake who'd betrayed her, it was the fact that Ethan didn't believe she was innocent. That was what hurt the most. If he didn't trust her, he certainly didn't love her. She'd been living in a fool's paradise, thinking his ardor might lead to love. Now she knew that it wouldn't. Desire was never enough to compensate for a lack of real feeling.

She pleaded a headache and spent the rest of the night in her room, even refusing supper. Having to watch Miriam gloat would be the last straw, and she had no stomach for any more arguments with Ethan. She knew from painful experience that once his mind was made up, nothing was going to change it. She'd have to leave in the morning. At least she did still have a little money and her credit cards. She could manage on that. She could go to a hotel.

Her eyes were red with tears. Damn Miriam! The other woman had found the perfect way to foul up everything. Now she'd have Ethan again, just as she'd planned. Well, Arabella thought viciously, they deserved each other. So much for all the pretense. Ethan had admitted that it had only been desire that he felt, that he'd pitied her and that's why he'd invited her here. Probably the excuse of keeping Miriam at bay had been fictitious—like his so-called impotence. She'd never

believe another word he said, she told herself firmly.
If they were quits, it was just fine with her. If Miriam
was what he wanted, he could have her. She put on her
gown, turned out the light, and lay down. Amazingly,
she slept.

Coreen finally found five minutes alone with her
son, Miriam having given in to drowsiness and gone to
bed.

"Can I bring you anything?" Coreen asked him. "We
didn't have a proper supper. Arabella went to bed hours
ago with a headache."

"Too bad," Ethan said coldly.

Coreen scowled at him. "What's eating you? Come
on, out with it!"

"Miriam phoned the house before you and Arabella
left for Houston to tell you I needed a ride to the
hospital," he said curtly. "Arabella didn't even bother
to tell you. Apparently the shopping trip meant more
than any little injury of mine."

Coreen gaped at him. "What are you talking about?
There was only one phone call and it was from Arabella's
father!"

"Is that what she told you?" he asked with a hard
laugh. "Did you talk to him, or hear him? Did Betty
Ann?"

Coreen moved close to the bed, her eyes full of
disapproval and concern. "I had hoped that you cared
about Arabella," she said. "I hoped that you'd be able to
see through Miriam's glitter this time to the cold, selfish
woman underneath. Perhaps that kind of woman really

appeals to you because you're as incapable of real love as she is."

Ethan's eyebrows went straight up. "I beg your pardon?"

"You heard me. I don't need proof that Arabella didn't lie. She wouldn't walk away and leave an injured animal, much less an injured person. I believe that because I know her, because I care about her." She stared down at him. "Love and trust are two sides of one coin, Ethan. If you can believe Arabella capable of such a cold-blooded act, then I'd suggest that you forget marriage and put Miriam's ring back through your nose. God knows, right now I think the two of you deserve each other."

She turned and left him there. He picked up a cup from the table and slammed it furiously at the closed door. He knew he was fuddled, but his mother had no right to say things like that to him. Why would Miriam lie about a phone call that he could certainly check? All he had to do was get the record of where the call originated from the phone company to prove a lie. Anyway, Miriam had been different lately, very caring and warm, and he'd actually enjoyed her company. He knew all about the man she was in love with, and he'd done his best to encourage her to go back to the Caribbean and try again. So that meant she wasn't interested in him as a man anymore, and it gave her no reason to try and break up his apparent romance with Arabella.

Or was it all a ruse on Miriam's part to get him back? Could Arabella be innocent of what he'd accused her of? He didn't want to think about that, because if she was, he'd just ruined everything. Again. He groaned. It was the way Arabella had dressed, the things she'd said about getting an expensive wedding gown, and then the way it had hurt when Miriam said Arabella was going to Houston anyway, despite his condition.

He was concussed and his mind wasn't working properly. He'd been sure that Arabella loved him, but when Miriam said she wouldn't come to see about him, he thought he'd been mistaken. Then he'd worked himself into a lather thinking that she'd only wanted to use him, as Miriam once had. Miriam had been so different lately that he'd been sure she'd changed, that she wasn't the same self-seeking woman she had been. But was she different? Or was he just susceptible because his head was throbbing and Arabella had hurt him?

He lay down and closed his eyes. He wouldn't—he couldn't—think about that right now. He'd think about it in the morning, instead, when his throbbing head was a little clearer. Then he'd face the future, if he still had one with Arabella.

Chapter Nine

Arabella woke to the sound of voices the next morning. She sat up in bed, her pale blue gown twisted around her slender body, her long brown hair a tangle around her shoulders, just as Mary knocked briefly then opened the door, rushing inside.

"Hello!" she said, laughing, as she hugged Arabella and placed a bag of souvenir items on the bed. Mary was tan and relaxed and looked lovely. "These are all for you," she said. "T-shirts, shell things, necklaces, skirts, and even a few postcards. Did you miss me?"

"Oh, Mary, yes, I did," Arabella said with a long sigh, hugging her back. Mary was the best, and the only, real friend she'd ever had. "Things are getting so complicated."

"I heard you and Ethan are going to be married," Mary continued, all eyes.

Arabella's face fell. "Yes. Well, that was just what we told Miriam. The wedding is off."

"But your gown!" Mary protested, nodding toward the box in the armchair. "Coreen told us all about it."

"It's going back today," Arabella said firmly. "Ethan broke off the engagement last night. He wants Miriam back."

Mary sat very still. "He what?"

"Wants Miriam back," Arabella said quietly. "She's changed, or so he says. They've gotten real thick in the past couple of days." Which was odd, she told herself, because she herself had gotten real thick with Ethan in the past couple of days. She felt sick all over. "And I'm leaving," she added, giving in to a decision she'd made the night before. "I hate to ask when you're just off the plane, but could you drive me into Jacobsville later?"

Mary almost refused, but the look in her friend's eyes killed all her hopeful words. Whatever had happened, Arabella had been terribly hurt by it. "All right," she said with a forced smile. "I'll be glad to. Does Ethan know you're going?"

"Not yet," Arabella said. "He doesn't need to. He fell yesterday and got concussed." She had to bite back all her concern for him. She couldn't afford to let it show. "He's all right. Miriam's taking care of him, and that's the way he wants it. He said so."

Mary knew there had to be more to it than that, but she kept her silence. "I'll let you dress and pack. I gather that I'm not to tell anyone you're going?"

"Please."

"All right. Come downstairs when you're ready."

"I'll do that. Could you…take that with you?" she asked, nodding toward the box.

Mary picked it up, thinking privately that it was a pity Ethan had waited until she bought the dress to call off the wedding. He didn't seem to care very much for Arabella's feelings, either, because she was obviously crushed.

"I'll see you directly," Arabella said as Mary went out and closed the door.

She got dressed, minus the bra that she still couldn't fasten, in a suit with a thick jacket that she buttoned up. She packed her few things with her good hand and tied a scarf around her neck to hold the cast at her waist. It got heavy when she moved around very much. She picked up her suitcase, then, after a final glance in the mirror at her pale face without makeup, left the room where she'd been so happy and so sad.

There was one last thing she wanted to do. She had to say goodbye to Ethan. She wouldn't admit, even to herself, how much she hoped he'd changed his mind.

Actually, at that moment, Ethan was having a long talk with a quiet and dejected Miriam. He'd asked for the truth, and she'd reluctantly given it to him, her conscience pricked by the conversation that Ethan didn't know she'd had with Arabella the night before.

"I shouldn't have done it," she told him, smiling mistily. "You've been so different, and I saw the way things could have been if you'd loved me when we first married. I knew I didn't stand a chance against Arabella, so I had other men to get even," she confessed for the first time. She met his eyes apologetically. "You should have married her. I'm sorry I made things difficult for you. And I'm very sorry about the lie I told yesterday."

Ethan was having trouble breathing properly. All he

could think of was what he'd said to Arabella the night before. He'd been out of his muddled head with anger.

"I called off the wedding," he said absently, and winced.

"She'll forgive you," Miriam said sadly. "I'm sure she feels the same way about you." She reached out and touched his face. "I do love my Jared, you know." She sighed. "I ran because of the baby. I thought he wouldn't want it, but now I'm not so sure. I could at least give him the benefit of the doubt, I suppose. I didn't sleep last night thinking about it. I'll phone him this morning and see what develops."

"You may find he wants the baby as much as you do," he replied. He smiled at her. "I'm glad we can part as friends."

"So am I," she said fervently. "Not that I deserve it. I know I've been a royal pain in the neck."

"Not so much anymore," he assured her.

"I'll go and make that call. Thank you, Ethan, for everything. I'm so sorry about what I did. You deserve more than I ever gave you." She bent and kissed him with warm tenderness.

He reached up, giving her back the kiss, for old times' sake. A kiss of parting, between friends, with no sexual overtones.

That was what Arabella saw when she stopped in the open door. A kiss that wasn't sexual and held such exquisite tenderness that it made her feel like a voyeur. She knew she'd gone white. So it was that way. They'd reconciled. Miriam loved him and now they were going to remarry and live happily ever after. Miriam had won.

She smiled bitterly and retraced her steps so that they didn't even know she'd been in the room.

She ran into Coreen going down the staircase.

"I'm just on my way to see Ethan…." She stopped dead, staring at Arabella's suitcase.

"Mary's driving me to town," Arabella said, her voice a little wobbly. "And I wouldn't disturb Ethan just now, if I were you. He's rather involved with Miriam."

"Oh, this is getting completely out of hand!" Coreen said harshly. "Why won't he listen?"

"He's in love with her, Coreen," the younger woman said. "He can't help that, you know. He said last night that it was really only out of pity that he asked me here. He wanted me, but he loves Miriam. It would never have worked. It's best that I leave now, so that I won't be an embarrassment to him."

"My dear," Coreen said miserably. She hugged Arabella warmly. "You know the door is always open. I'll miss you."

"I'll miss you, too. Mary was going to take the dress back to the store for me, but…but Miriam might like it," she said bravely. "All it would need is a little alteration."

"I'll take care of the dress," Coreen said. "Will you be all right? Where will you go?"

"I'll go to a motel for the time being. I'll phone my father when I've settled in. Don't worry, I've got money, thanks to Ethan's intervention. I won't go hungry, and I can take care of myself. But thank you for all you've done for me. I'll never forget you."

"I'll never forget you either, darling," Coreen said quietly. "Keep in touch, won't you?"

"Of course," Arabella lied with a smile. That was the very last thing she intended doing now, for Ethan's sake.

She followed Mary out to the car after exchanging

farewells with Betty Ann and a puzzled Matt. She didn't even look back as the car wound down the driveway to the road.

Just as Arabella was going out to the car, Miriam was lifting her head and smiling at Ethan. "Not bad. I'm sorry we didn't make it. Shall I go downstairs and explain it all to Arabella and your mother?" she asked with a grimace. "I guess they'll pitch me out the back door on my head when I get through."

"It's my head that's going to be in danger, I'm afraid," he said ruefully. "No, I'll handle it. You'd better go and call your Caribbean connection."

"I'll do that. Thanks."

He watched her go, and lay back against the pillows. He'd heard Matt and Mary come in and he was waiting for them to come and say hello. Maybe he could get Arabella up here and try to sort things out before it was too late. He heard a car door slam twice and an engine rev up, and he frowned. Surely Mary and Matt weren't leaving already.

Minutes later, a coldly furious Coreen walked into his room and glared at him.

"Well, I hope you're happy," she told him. "You've got what you wanted. She just left."

He sat up, scowling at her. "Who just left?" he asked with a chilling sense of loss.

"Arabella," Coreen informed him. "She said you'd called off the wedding. She left her dress for Miriam and said to congratulate you on your forthcoming remarriage."

"Oh, for God's sake!" he burst out. He threw his legs off the bed and tried to get up, but his head was still spinning with the aftereffects of the day before. He sat down again and rubbed his forehead. "I'm not marrying Miriam! Where in hell did she get that idea?"

"From you, I suppose, after the bite you apparently took out of her last night. And something must have been going on in here when she left, because she said you and Miriam were involved when she came downstairs."

She'd seen Miriam kiss him. He remembered the kiss, realized how it would look to an outsider, and he groaned out loud. "My God, I've got a knack for ruining my life," he said with a rough sigh. "I must have a deep-buried death wish. Where did she go?"

"To a motel, she said. Mary will know which one."

He lifted his head, and his eyes were anguished. "She'll call her father," he said. "He'll be here like a shot to take her over again."

"Do remember who pushed her out of the door, won't you, dear boy?" his mother asked with smiling venom.

"I thought she'd deserted me!" he burst out.

"As if Arabella would do any such thing," she scoffed. "How could you have believed it?"

"Because I had a concussion and I was half out of my head," he returned angrily.

"And what did she see on her way out that convinced her Miriam needed the wedding gown?" Coreen added.

"I kissed her. She kissed me," he corrected. He threw up his hands. "Miriam's going back to the Caribbean to marry the father of her child, if everything works out all right," he said. "It was a goodbye kiss."

"You fool," Coreen said evenly. "Four years ago, you put Arabella's welfare above your own. You married the wrong woman and cheated her as well as yourself, and now you've thrown away the second chance you might have had. Why didn't you tell Arabella how you feel about her!"

He lowered his eyes. Some things he couldn't share, even with his mother. "She's career-minded. She always was. She came here because she was hurt and needed some security. She was reluctant from the first when I tried to get her to marry me. I think she was afraid that she'd be able to play again and be stuck here with me."

"More likely she was afraid you were just using her as a blind for the feelings you had for Miriam," Coreen replied. "She said you only wanted her, but you loved Miriam. She believed it."

Ethan sighed heavily and lay back down. "I'll go after her, when I get my head together."

"Never mind," Coreen said. "She won't come back. She's let you cut up her heart twice already. She won't risk it again."

His eyes opened. "What do you mean, cut up her heart?"

"Ethan," she said patiently, "she was in love with you four years ago. Desperately in love. She thought Miriam just wanted what you had, not you. She was trying to protect you, but you accused her of interfering and God knows what else. She ran then, too, and kept running. Didn't you ever wonder why she arranged to come here to see Jan, and later Mary, only when she knew you wouldn't be here?"

"No, because I was too busy making sure I didn't have to see her," he said doggedly. He averted his eyes. "It hurt too much. I was married, Miriam wouldn't divorce me…." His broad shoulders rose and fell. "I couldn't bear the torment of seeing her and not being able to touch her honorably." He looked up at his mother. "How do you know how she felt about me?" he asked.

"It's obvious," she said simply. "She chose music as a substitute, just as you chose Miriam. You're both fools. What a horrible waste of time."

Ethan was inclined to agree. So Arabella had loved him. He lay back down and closed his eyes, trying to imagine how it would have been if he'd given up his plans to save her from what he thought would have been a mistake, if he'd married her instead. They'd have children by now, they'd be a family. Arabella would sleep in his arms every night and love him. He couldn't bear the images that haunted him. He'd driven her away a second time with his idiotic accusations, and now he'd probably never be able to get her back. He heard his mother leave, but he didn't bother to open his eyes.

Arabella got a room in a downtown Jacobsville motel. There were several to choose from, but her favorite was an adobe-style one with a Spanish flavor. She settled into her room, trying not to think how bare and austere and impersonal it was compared to the one she'd had at the Hardeman ranch.

Mary hadn't wanted to leave her there, but she'd insisted. She couldn't stay in the house now that she knew how it was between Ethan and Miriam. It was too painful. A clean break was best. She picked up the phone when she'd unpacked and phoned her father in Dallas. The cast came off in nine days. Her father would meet her here then and they'd go back to Houston. He'd sublet their apartment there while he was in Dallas, but they could get another temporarily. Odd that it didn't even bother her to think about being back with her parent again. She didn't feel intimidated anymore.

Time went by slowly. Mary came to visit, but Arabella was reluctant to listen to any news from the ranch, especially about Ethan. She didn't want to hear what was going on at the house, it would be too painful. The only reality was that Ethan hadn't bothered to call or come by or even drop her a postcard, even though he knew by now—or so Mary had said before Arabella protested listening to news of Ethan—that Miriam had lied about the phone call. He knew, but he wouldn't apologize for the things he'd said. He never apologized, she reflected. Since Miriam was still with him, why should he bother? He and Arabella were now past history.

Meanwhile, Ethan was trying to come to grips with his own idiocy. He was certain that Arabella wouldn't listen to him. He couldn't blame her; he'd certainly been eloquent in his condemnation. He thought it would be better if he let things cool down for a few days before they had a showdown. In the meantime, Miriam's man was on his way up to Texas. They'd reconciled and Miriam had been on a cloud ever since, barely coherent except when she was talking about the planter she was going to marry. Ethan enjoyed her company, especially now that he was well and truly off the hook, now that he was able to understand the past and why things had happened the way they had. Miriam had suffered an unfortunate experience with a family friend as a child. As a result, she'd become brittle in her dealings with men, and very hostile toward them. Only now, secure in her pregnancy and the love of her planter, was she able to come to grips with the past that had made her what she was when she'd married Ethan.

Ethan's only regret was that he'd married her in the first place. It had been unfair to her, to Arabella and even to himself. He should have followed his instincts, which were to marry Arabella and let the chips fall where they may. He'd never been able to give Miriam anything except the dregs of his desires for another woman and, eventually, not even that. He hadn't understood that Miriam's childhood had made it impossible for her to give herself wholly to any man. She'd been looking for love in a series of impossible physical liaisons that were only briefly satisfying. She'd wanted Ethan's love, but he'd withheld it, and she'd tried to punish him. Arabella, though, had suffered as well, trapped in a career that her father controlled, with no hope of escape.

It had thrilled him when Coreen had told him Arabella had once loved him. But he didn't know what she felt now. She probably hated him. He'd started for town three times in the past several days, but he'd stopped. She needed time. So did he.

Mary came up the steps as he was going down them, and he stopped her, trying not to look as unhappy as he felt.

"How is she?" he asked bluntly, because he was certain she'd been to see her friend.

"Lonely," Mary said, her voice gentle. "The cast comes off Tuesday."

"Yes." He stared off over the tree-lined horizon. "Is her father here yet?"

"He'll be here Tuesday." Mary was nervous of Ethan, but she hesitated. "She won't talk about you," she said. "She doesn't look well."

He glanced down at her with flashing silver eyes.

"Nobody told her to leave," he said cuttingly, stung by the remark.

"How could she stay, knowing that you're going to marry Miriam all over again?" she asked. "I guess you two do deserve each other," she added with the first show of spirit Ethan had ever seen in her, and she was gone before he could correct her impression of the situation.

What made everyone think Miriam was marrying him? He sighed angrily as he went down the steps. Probably because neither of them had told the rest of the family what was going on. Well, when her planter arrived they'd get the picture. For now, he couldn't let himself dwell on how bad Arabella looked. If he thought about it long enough, he was sure he'd go stark, raving mad.

Mary and Matt had studiously ignored Miriam since Arabella's departure, and Coreen had been so coldly polite to the woman that she might as well have had icicles dripping off her. Ethan tried to make up for his family, which only reinforced their speculation about Miriam's status in his life.

Miriam's intended and Arabella's father arrived in town at the same time. While Jared was being introduced to the Hardemans, Arabella was having the cast off and being told that her hand and wrist had healed almost to perfection. Her father had beamed at the specialist. But only at first.

"Almost to perfection," Dr. Wagner repeated, frowning at Arabella's father. "Translated, that means that Miss Craig will play the piano again. Unfortunately it also means that she will never regain her former mastery. Severed tendons are never the same when they heal, for the primary reason that they're shortened by the process of reattaching them. I'm sorry."

Arabella didn't realize how much she'd been counting on favorable prognosis. She collapsed into tears.

Her father forgot his own disappointment when he saw hers. Clumsily, he took her in his arms and held her, patting her ineffectually on the back while he murmured words of comfort.

He took her out to dinner that night. She dressed in her one good cocktail dress, black with a scattering of sequins, and knotted her long hair at her nape. She looked elegant, but even with the unwieldy cast off, she felt dowdy. The skin that had been under the cast was unnaturally pale and there were scars. But she kept her hand in her lap and in the dark atmosphere of the restaurant and lounge, she was certain that nobody noticed.

"What will we do?" Arabella asked quietly.

Her father sighed. "Well, for now, I'll see about releasing some of the new recordings and re-releasing the older ones." He looked across the table at her. "I haven't been much of a father, have I? Deserting you after the wreck…I guess you thought I didn't want you without a career to keep us up."

"Yes, I did," she confessed.

"The wreck brought back your mother's accident," he said. It was a subject he'd never discussed before, but she sensed that he was getting something off his chest. "Arabella, she died because I had one drink too many at a party. I was driving, and my reaction time was down. Oh, there were no charges," he said with a cold laugh when he saw her expression. "I wasn't even legally drunk. But the police knew, and I knew, that I could have reacted quicker and avoided the other car. She died instantly. I've lived with that guilt for so long." He leaned back in his chair, making patterns in the condensation on his water glass. "I couldn't admit my mistake. I buried the past in my mind and concentrated on you. I was going to be noble, I was going to dedicate my life to your talent, to your glorious career." He studied her wan face. "But you didn't want a career, did you? You wanted Ethan Hardeman."

"And he wanted Miriam, so what difference does it make now? In fact," she added without looking at him, "Miriam is back and they're reconciling."

"I'm sorry," he said. He studied her. "You know, the wreck brought it all back," he continued. "Your mother's death, trying to cope without her, trying to live with my guilt." He studied his locked-together fingers on the table. "You needed me and I couldn't bear to face you. I came so close to losing you the way I lost her…."

His voice broke and Arabella suddenly saw her father as a man. Just a man, with all the fears and failings of any other human. It shocked her to realize that he wasn't omnipotent. Parents always seemed to be, somehow.

"I didn't remember how Mama died," she said, searching for words. "And I certainly didn't blame you for our wreck. There was nothing you could have done. Really," she emphasized when he lifted tormented eyes to hers. "Dad, I don't blame you."

He bit his lower lip hard and looked away. "Well, I blamed me," he said. "I called Ethan because there was no one else, but I thought in a way, it might make up to you what I'd cheated you out of. I figured with your hand in that shape, Ethan might decide to stop being noble and give you a chance."

"Thank you," she said gently. "But all Ethan wants is his ex-wife. Maybe that's just as well. Four years ago, I worshipped the ground he walked on, but I'm older now...."

"And still in love with him," he finished for her. He shook his head. "All my efforts backfired, didn't they? All right, Arabella. What do you want to do now?"

She was amazed that he was asking her opinion. It was a first—like realizing that he was human and fallible. She liked him much better this way. It was a whole new relationship, because he was treating her like an adult for the first time. "Well, I don't want to stay in Jacobsville," she said firmly. "The sooner we can leave here, the better."

"I guess I'll have to go to Houston and find a place, first," he said. "Then I'll see what I can do about finding myself a job." He waved aside her objections. "I've spent altogether too much time in the past. You have a right to your own life. I'm only sorry that it took another near-fatal wreck to bring me to my senses."

Arabella slid her hand into his and clasped it warmly. "You've been very good to me, Dad," she said gently. "I don't have any complaints."

"Are you sure about Miriam?" he asked with a frown. "Because I don't believe Ethan really wanted to marry her in the first place. And I know he was damned near crazy when I phoned him about you being hurt in the wreck."

"I'm sure," she said, closing the book on that subject forever.

He relented. "All right. We'll start again. And don't worry about that hand," he added. "You can always teach, if everything else fails." He smiled at her gently.

"There's a great deal of satisfaction in seeing someone you've coached become famous. Take my word for it."

She smiled at him. "I can live with that," she said. Inwardly, she was almost relieved. She loved to play the piano, but she'd never wanted the tours, the endless road trips, the concerts. Now they were gone forever, and she wasn't really sorry.

Her father left the next morning for Houston in the car he'd rented for the trip to Jacobsville. Arabella was lazy, not rising until late morning. She decided to have lunch in the restaurant and went early.

Their seafood was delicious, so she ordered that and settled back to wait for it.

Incredible how her life had changed, she thought as she came to grips finally with what the surgeon had told her about her hand. What could have been traumatic wasn't that at all. She accepted it with relative ease. Of course, her father's new attitude had helped.

She felt a shadow fall over her and turned with an automatic smile to face the waiter. But it wasn't a waiter. It was Ethan Hardeman.

Chapter Ten

Arabella schooled her features not to show any of the emotions she was feeling. She stared up at him with a blank expression, while her poor heart ran wild and fed on the sight of him.

"Hello, Ethan," she said. "Nice to see you. Is Miriam with you?" she added with a pointed glance behind him.

He put his hat on an empty seat and lowered himself into the chair beside hers. "Miriam is getting married."

"Yes, I know," she began.

So Mary had already told her, he thought. That wasn't surprising, Mary came to see her almost every day. He caught eyes, but she quickly lowered her gaze to the beige sport coat he was wearing with dark slacks, a white silk shirt and striped tie.

He toyed with the utensils at his place. "I wanted to

come sooner, but I thought you needed a little time to yourself. What did the doctor say about your hand?" he added.

She managed to disguise her broken heart very well. To save her pride, she was going to have to lay it on thick. She couldn't let him know her predicament. Besides, he was getting married, and she wished the best for him. He didn't need her problems to mar his happiness. "It's fine," she said. "I have to have a little physical therapy and then I'm back to New York, by way of Houston, to take up where I left off."

His face hardened. He couldn't help it. He'd thought for certain that she'd never use that hand again, knowing how much damage had been done to it. Of course, these days they had all sorts of methods of repairing damaged tendons, so maybe there was a new technique. But it didn't help his pride. He'd left things too late. If he'd told her how he felt at the beginning, if he'd revealed his feelings, things might have been different. His whole life seemed to be falling apart, and all because of his lousy timing.

He stared at her across the table. "Then you've got what you want," he said.

"Yes. But so have you," she reminded him with a forced smile. "I hope you and Miriam will be very happy. I really do, Ethan."

He gaped at her. Meanwhile, the waiter appeared with her salad and paused to ask Ethan if he was ready to order. Absently, he ordered a steak and salad and coffee and sat back heavily in the chair when the man left.

"Arabella, I'm not getting married."

She blinked. "You said you were."

"I said Miriam was."

"What's the difference?" she asked.

He sighed heavily. "She's marrying a man she met down in the Caribbean," he said. "He's the father of her child."

"Oh." She watched the way he twirled his water glass, his eyes downcast, his face heavily lined. "Ethan, I'm so sorry," she said gently. She reached out hesitantly and touched one of his hands.

Electric current shot through him. He lifted his eyes to catch hers while his fingers linked around and through her own. He'd missed her more than he even wanted to admit. The house, and his life, had been empty without her. "Care to console me?" he asked half seriously. "She and her fiancé are staying for a few days." He lowered his eyes to their linked hands so that she wouldn't see the hunger in them. "You could come back with me and help me bluff it out until they leave."

She closed her eyes briefly. "I can't."

"Why not? It's only for a couple of days. You could have your old room. Coreen and Mary would enjoy your company."

She weakened, but her pride was still smarting from the beating it had taken. "I shouldn't, Ethan."

His fingers tightened. "Will it help if I apologize?" he asked quietly. "I never meant to be so rough on you. I should have known better, but I was half out of my mind and I swallowed everything Miriam said."

"I thought you knew me better than that," she said sadly. "I suppose you have to love people to trust them, though."

He flinched. He felt as if he'd had a stake put through his heart. Yes, he should have trusted her. He hadn't, and now she was running away because he'd hurt her.

He couldn't let her get away from him now. No matter what it took.

"Listen, honey," he said softly, coaxing her eyes up to his, "it's been hard on all of us, having Miriam around. But she'll be gone soon."

Taking his heart with her, Arabella thought. She wished, oh, how she wished, that he could love her. "My father and I are going to Houston as soon as he finds a place for us," she said.

His jaw clenched. He hadn't counted on that complication, although he should have expected it. She had her career to think of, and that was her father's grubstake. "You could stay with us until he finds one," he said curtly.

"I'm happy here in the motel," she protested.

"Well, I'm not happy with you here," he said, his own voice arctic. His eyes began to kindle with feeling. "It's my fault you left. We were off to a good start, until I started jumping to conclusions."

"That's just as well." She searched his face. "I guess it's pretty painful for you. Losing her again."

"If you only knew," he replied, his voice deep and slow, but he wasn't thinking of Miriam. He brought her fingers to his lips and nibbled at them, watching the reaction color her face and bring a soft, helpless light to her green eyes. "Come home with me," he said. "You can sprawl across my bed in that satin gown and we'll make love again."

"Hush!" she exclaimed, looking around to make sure they weren't overheard.

"You're blushing."

"Of course I'm blushing. I want to forget that it ever

happened!" she muttered. She tried to draw her fingers away, but he held them tightly.

"We could give Miriam and her intended a grand send-off," he coaxed. "By the time she left, she'd be convinced that I didn't have a broken heart."

"And why should I want to do you another favor?" she demanded.

He looked her right in the eye. "I can't think of a single reason," he confessed with a warm, quiet smile. "But I hope you'll come, all the same. Maybe I can make up for the way I treated you."

Her fingers jerked in his and she went scarlet. "By making love to me again? Do you think I care so much that I'll be grateful for any crumbs left over from your relationship with Miriam?" she asked bluntly.

"No. I don't think that at all." He held her gaze, trying to find any sign that she still cared, that he hadn't quite ruined everything. That he might have one last chance before she resumed her career to make her understand how deeply involved his feelings were, how much he cared.

"I've heard you play." He lowered his eyes to her hands, caressing them gently. "You have genius in your hands. I'm glad you haven't lost that talent, Arabella, even if it means that I have to let you go again." And he might, but now he had the hope that it might not be a permanent loss this time. If he could convince her that he cared, she might yet come back to him one day.

She wanted to tell him. She started to tell him, to draw him out, to try to make him tell her if wanting was all he felt. But the waiter arrived with their order, and the moment was lost. She couldn't find the nerve to reopen the subject, especially when he started talking about Miriam's husband-to-be and the way he'd come dashing across the sea to get her.

After lunch, Ethan waited while she packed and left a message at the desk for her father to call her at the Hardeman ranch. Going back was against her better judgment, but she couldn't resist the temptation. In the long years ahead, at least she'd have a few bittersweet memories.

He drove her out to the ranch, his eyes thoughtful, his face quiet and brooding.

"Roundup's over," he announced as they sped down the road out of Jacobsville. "It feels good to have a little free time."

"I imagine so." She glanced off the highway at the massive feedlot that seemed to stretch forever toward the horizon. "Do the Ballenger brothers still own that feedlot?"

"They certainly do," he mused, following her glance. "Calhoun and Justin are making a mint on it. Good thing, too, the way they're procreating. Calhoun and Abby have a son and a daughter and Justin and Shelby have two sons."

"What ever happened to Shelby's brother, Tyler?" she asked absently.

"Tyler married an Arizona girl. They don't have any kids yet, but their dude ranch just made headlines— Tyler and his wife have expanded it to include a whole authentic Old-West adobe village as a tourist attraction, and they've enlarged their tourist facilities. It looks as if they're going to make a mint, too."

"Good for them," Arabella said. She stared down at the floorboard of the car. "It's nice to hear about local people making good."

"That's what we thought about you," he said, "when you started making headlines. We all knew you had the talent."

"But not the ambition," she confessed. "My father had that, for both of us. I only loved music. I still do."

"Well, you'll be on your way again when you get the physical therapy out of the way, I guess," he said, his voice hardening.

"Of course," she mumbled numbly and moved her damaged hand to stare down at its whiteness. She flexed the muscles, knowing she'd never be the same again.

Ethan caught a glimpse of the expression on her face. It kept him puzzled and quiet all the way home.

Miriam and her fiancé were beaming like newlyweds. Even Coreen seemed to have warmed toward her, and Miriam went out of her way to make Arabella feel comfortable.

"I'm really sorry for messing things up between you and Ethan," the older woman said when she and Arabella were briefly alone during the long afternoon. In her newfound happiness, she could afford to be generous, and she'd seen the misery she'd caused Ethan already. "I was evening up old scores, but it wasn't Ethan's fault, or yours, that he couldn't love me." She glanced toward Jared, a tall, pleasant man with elegance and obvious breeding, and her face softened with emotion. "Jared is everything I dreamed of in a husband. I ran because I didn't think he'd want our child, as I did. My emotions were all over the place. I guess I had some wild idea of getting Ethan to marry me again to get even with Jared." She looked at Arabella with quiet apology. "I'm sorry. I hope this time you and Ethan will make a go of it."

That wasn't possible now, but it was kind of Miriam

to think, even belatedly, of Ethan's happiness. She managed a smile. "Thank you. I hope you'll be happy, too."

"I don't deserve it, but so do I," Miriam murmured. She smiled self-consciously and went back to her fiancé.

Mary was giving Arabella curious looks. Later on, she dragged her friend to one side.

"What's going on? You could have knocked me over with a feather when I saw Ethan walk in with you," she whispered. "Have you made up?"

"Not really. He wants me to help him put on a good front so Miriam won't think she's broken his heart," Arabella said, her eyes going to Ethan like homing pigeons.

Mary watched the look and smiled secretly. "I don't think she could get that impression, not considering the way he's been sneaking looks at you ever since he brought you in."

Arabella laughed halfheartedly. "He's just putting on an act," she said.

"Is that what it's called?" Mary murmured dryly. "Well, ignore it while you can."

"I thought I was…." Her voice trailed off as she encountered a long, simmering gaze from Ethan's silver eyes and got lost in the fierce hunger in them. The rest of the people seemed to vanish. She didn't look away and neither did he, and electricity sizzled between them for one long, achingly sweet minute. Then Coreen diverted his attention and Arabella was able to breathe again.

For the remainder of the day, he didn't leave the house. After supper, while the rest of the family watched a movie in the living room on the VCR, Arabella excused herself and changed into comfortable jeans and a white tank top before she sneaked back downstairs and went into the library to try the piano for the first time since the wreck.

She closed the door quietly, so that no one would hear her. She positioned the piano bench carefully and sat down, easing up the cover over the keyboard. It was a grand piano, because Coreen played herself, and it was in perfect tune. She touched middle C and ran a scale one octave lower with her left hand.

Very nice, she thought, smiling. Then she put her right hand on the keyboard. It trembled and the thumb protested when she tried to turn it under on F. She grimaced. All right, she thought after a minute. Perhaps scales would be just too difficult right now. Perhaps a simple piece would be easier.

She chose a Chopin nocturne, a beginner's piece she'd played in her early days at the piano. She began very slowly, but it made no difference. Her hand was lax and trembly and totally uncooperative. She groaned and her hands crashed down despairingly on the keyboard, seeing months of work ahead before she could even do a scale, perhaps years before she could play again normally, if at all.

She didn't hear Ethan come in. She didn't hear him close the door behind him and stand staring at her downbent head for a long time. He'd heard the crash of her hands on the piano and it had made him curious. He knew she was probably feeling frustrated, that it would take a long time for her hand to be able to stand the torment of long practice.

It was only when he came up to her and straddled the piano bench facing her that she looked up.

"You can't play," he said. He'd heard her from outside the door. He knew the truth now. She gritted her teeth, waiting for the blow to fall. "It will take time," he said. "Don't be impatient."

She let out a slow breath. So he didn't know. At least her pride was safe.

"That's right." She met his eyes and felt her heart drop. "So you don't have to feel sorry for me. I can still play, Ethan. I'll just need a little more time to heal, and then a lot of practice."

"Of course." He looked down at the keyboard. "Hurt, didn't it? What I said about feeling sorry for you."

"The truth is always the best way," she said numbly.

He shifted, his eyes pinning hers. "What are you and your father going to do until you're proficient again?"

"He's going to see about releasing some of my new recordings and re-releasing some of the older ones," she replied. Her left hand touched the keyboard reverently and she mourned fiercely the loss of her abilities. She couldn't even show it, couldn't cry her eyes out on Ethan's broad chest, because she didn't dare admit it to him. "So, you see, I won't have any financial worries right away. Dad and I will look after each other."

He drew in a short, angry breath. "Is he going to win again?" he asked coldly.

She drew away, puzzled by the fury in his tone. "Again?"

"I let him take you away from here once," he said, his jaw taut, his silver eyes flashing. "I let you walk away, because he convinced me that you needed him and music more than you needed me. But I can't do that again, Arabella."

She hesitated. "You...you loved Miriam."

His face hardened. "No."

"You only want me," she began again, searching his eyes while her heart threatened to run away with her. "And not enough to marry me."

"No."

He was confusing her. She pushed back her long, dark hair nervously. "Can't you say something besides just 'no'?" she asked slowly.

"Put your leg over here." He readjusted her so that she was facing him on the long, narrow piano bench. Then he pulled her jean-clad legs gently over his so that they were in the most intimate position they'd ever shared. His lean hands held her hips, pulling them hard into his, and then he looked down into her eyes and deliberately moved her so that she felt, with shocking emphasis, the slow arousal of his body.

Her nails dug into his shoulders. "Ethan, for heaven's sake!" she protested in shocked outrage.

But he held her there despite her struggles. His jaw was taut and his breathing unsteady. "I'll be damned if I'll let you go," he said huskily. "You're going to marry me."

She couldn't believe what she was hearing. The feel of him against her was making reason almost impossible, anyway.

"Say yes," he said, bending to her mouth. "Say it now, or so help me God, I'll have you where you sit!" His hands pulled her closer and she felt the physical reality of the threat.

"Yes, Ethan," she could manage that, barely. Not because she was afraid of him, but because she loved him too much to refuse him a second time. Then his lips were against hers and she was clinging to him like

ivy, only living through his mouth and his hands and
his body.

Somehow he managed to get his shirt and hers out
of the way, and she felt him from the waist up, bare
and hair-roughened muscles warm and hard against her
sensitive breasts while he kissed her until her mouth
ached. His strong hands slid up and down her back,
moving her in a new and shameless rhythm against his
thighs, making her moan with the intimacy of their
position.

"It will be like this in bed," he whispered, his deep
voice shaken as it made tiny chills against her moist,
swollen lips. "Except that we'll join in the most intimate
way of all first. Then I'll rock you against me…like
this…and we'll have each other on crisp, white sheets
in my bed…!"

His tongue penetrated her mouth. She arched against
him, moaning, her hands trembling as they caught in his
hair and held his mouth against her own. She could see
them—Ethan's lean, dark-skinned body over hers, the
light glistening on his damp skin, the movement of it
against her own pale flesh in a rhythm as deep, as slow,
as waves against the beach. His strained face above hers,
his breath shaking, as hers would be, his mouth moving
to her breasts…

She caught her breath. Sensations of pleasure made
her shudder as his hands clenched on her hips and forced
her even closer.

"I want you," he groaned against her mouth. His
fingers trembled as they slid under the waistband of
her jeans.

"I know," she whispered feverishly. Her hands slid
to his thighs, trembling too. "I want…you, too."

He shuddered with the fierce need to give in to what he was feeling, what she was feeling. But it couldn't happen like this. No, he told himself. No! He eased back a breath and looked down into her soft, misty eyes. "Not like this," he bit off. "Our first time shouldn't be on a piano bench in an unlocked room. Should it?"

She stared up at him, shivering. It had only then occurred to her where they were. "I saw us," she whispered unsteadily. "In bed."

His face clenched. "My God, so did I, twisting against each other in a fever so hot it burned." He buried his face in her throat, and it was burning hot. His arms contracted.

His hands smoothed against her bare back and he touched her soft breasts. He lifted his head, looking down at the rose-tipped softness in his hands. "Did you ever dream that we'd be like this together one day?" he asked, almost in awe, and lifted his eyes to hold hers. "Sitting alone in a quiet room with your body open to my eyes and my hands, and so natural that we both accepted it without embarrassment?"

"I dreamed of it," she confessed in a soft whisper. She looked down at the darkness of his hands against the creamy beauty of her breasts. She trembled, and didn't mind letting him see. She belonged to him now. If wanting was all he felt, she could live with it. She'd have to.

"So did I," he whispered huskily. "Every long, lonely night." And he bent to take one small, perfect breast into his mouth.

She arched to him, clinging to his hair, gasping at the delicious sensations that washed over her, loving the warm moist suction of his mouth on her.

"It will be like this in bed, too," he whispered against her flushed skin. "Except that I'll kiss more than your breasts this way, and I won't stop until you're as satisfied as I am."

She drew her mouth over his eyes, his cheekbones, his nose, his mouth. "I hope you won't be sorry," she said quietly.

He lifted his head and looked down at her. If she'd ever loved him, he'd killed it. He was bulldozing her into this wedding, but it seemed the only way out. Perhaps love could be taught. "We'll have a white wedding, with all the trimmings," he added. "Complete with a wedding night. There won't be any anticipating our vows, and to hell with modern attitudes." He kissed her gently. "This is what marriage should be. A good marriage, with respect on both sides and honor to make it all perfect."

Respect. Honor. No mention of love, but perhaps she was being greedy. "Your mother was right. You are a puritan," she teased.

"So are you." He lifted her away from him with rueful reluctance and fastened her clothes again, then his. "I like the idea of a blushing, shy bride," he murmured, watching her face color. "Do you mind?"

"No," she assured him. "Not at all. I've waited so long to be one."

"As long as I've waited for you," he replied, his face almost a stranger's with its hard restraint. He moved away from her. "We'll make it together this time," he said. "Despite your father and Miriam and all the other obstacles, this time we'll make it."

She looked up at him with hope and quiet adoration. "Yes. This time we'll make it," she whispered.

They had to. She knew that she'd never survive having to leave him again. Later, she'd explain about her father and the peace they'd made. For now, it was enough that they were facing a future with each other. Love might come later, if she could be the kind of wife he wanted, and needed. In the meantime, she'd live one day at a time.

Her only worry was what he was going to think if he found out that her career was over. He might think again that she was marrying him for security.

She phoned her father that night and explained the situation to him. Oddly enough, he wasn't disappointed, and he even congratulated her. He'd make do, he promised, and she'd get the lion's share of the deals he was working on her behalf.

That reassured her. She'd have her little nest egg. Then, in the future, when Ethan finally tired of her body, she'd have something to fall back on. She could have a kind of life, even though it wouldn't include him.

She slept fitfully, wondering if she'd made the right decision. Was it right for Ethan, who was losing the woman he really loved? Or should she have let him go for good? By morning, she was no closer to a decision.

Chapter Eleven

"So it's back on again," Coreen said with a nod, eyeing her son warily as he and a somber Arabella broke the news to her. "Uh-huh. For how long this time?"

"For good." He lifted his chin. "You took the gown back, I suppose," he added.

"No, I didn't take the gown back," Coreen replied. "I stuck it in the closet because I was reasonably sure that you inherited enough of my common sense not to duplicate the worst mistake of your life."

He stared at her. "You kept it?"

"Yes." She smiled at Arabella. "I hoped he'd come to his senses. I just wasn't sure that he could get past his old doubts. Especially," she added, with a grim glance in Miriam's direction, "when the past started to interfere with the present."

"I'll tell you all about that, someday," Ethan promised

his mother. "In the meantime, how about those plans for the wedding?"

"I'll call Shelby tonight. Is that all right with you, Arabella?"

"I'd like that," Arabella said with downcast eyes. "Are you sure Shelby will have time to help us?"

"She'll make it. Her mother and I were best friends, many years ago. This time, don't let Arabella get away," Coreen cautioned her son.

He looked down at Arabella with open hunger. "Not on your life. Not this time."

Arabella was trying not to look as nervous as she felt. That hunger in Ethan's eyes was real, even if he didn't love her, and she was suddenly uncertain about being able to satisfy it. If it hadn't dimmed in four years, how was she, a virgin, going to be woman enough to quench it?

He saw that fear in her eyes and misinterpreted it. He drew her to one side, scowling. "You aren't getting cold feet?"

"It's a big step, marriage," she said, hedging. "I'll get my nerve back."

"I'll give you anything you want," he said curtly. "You can have the moon, if you like."

She averted her gaze to Miriam and her fiancé. They looked the picture of coming nuptial bliss. Nothing like Arabella and Ethan, so tense and nervous with each other, stepping gingerly around the big issues they still had to face.

"I don't want the moon," she said. "I'll settle for a good marriage."

"We come from similar backgrounds and we have a lot in common," he said stubbornly. "We'll make it."

* * *

Shelby Jacobs Ballenger came by the next morning to talk to Arabella while Coreen and Mary listened in. She was a beautiful woman, much prettier than Miriam, and there had been a lot of gossip about the rocky romance she and her husband, Justin, had weathered. If it was true, none of it showed on her supremely happy face, and even the birth of two sons hadn't ruined her slender figure.

"I can't tell you how much we appreciate your help," Arabella said, smiling at Shelby. "I've never had to worry about arrangements of this sort before."

"It's my pleasure," Shelby replied, beaming. "I have a special place in my heart for weddings. My own was something to remember—unfortunately, for all the wrong reasons. But even with a bad start, it's been a miracle of togetherness. Justin is all I ever wanted, he and my boys."

"How do you manage any free time?" Arabella asked.

"It's not easy, with preschoolers," Shelby laughed, "but my sister-in-law is a jewel. Abby's keeping them while she's confined to the house. It's their third child on the way, you know. Justin said he was going to have a long talk with Calhoun and see if he knew what was causing them!"

Everyone laughed. It was well known around Jacobsville that Calhoun and Abby would have loved an even dozen.

"Now." Shelby got out a notebook. "Let me run you through the possibilities and then we'll sort out the particulars."

It took the better part of the morning. Shelby left

just before lunch and Arabella's head was swimming with it all.

"I don't want a wedding," she moaned to Coreen. "It's too complicated."

"We could elope," Ethan suggested.

Coreen glared at him. "Mary and Matt already did that. I won't let you. It's a church wedding or you'll live in sin!"

"Mother!" Ethan gave a theatrical expression of shock.

"It won't be that difficult. We already have the bride and the dress; all we have to worry about are invitations and food."

"Well, we could phone the guests and have a barbecue," he replied.

"Go away, Ethan," Coreen invited.

"Only if Arabella comes with me. I thought she might like to see the kittens. They've grown since she's been away," he added offhandedly.

She was tempted, but she wasn't sure she wanted to be alone with him. She'd successfully avoided him the night before, because of that look in his eyes that made her skin tingle.

"Come on, chicken," he taunted, so handsome in his jeans and chambray shirt that he looked the epitome of the movie cowboy.

"All right." She capitulated, following him out the door, to Coreen and Mary's amusement.

He caught her hand in his as they walked, linking her fingers sensuously through his own. He glanced down, his silver eyes approving of her gray slacks and gray-and-yellow patterned sweater. "You look good with your hair down like that."

She smiled. "It gets in my eyes."

He tilted his hat low over his eyes as they went out into the sunlight. "It's going to get hot today. We might go swimming."

"No, thanks," she said. Too quickly. She felt his eyes probing.

"Afraid history might repeat itself?" he asked softly. He stopped at the barn door and turned her, his hands gentle, his eyes questioning. "We're engaged. I might not draw back this time. I might take you."

She dropped her eyes to his chest. "I want a white wedding."

His own eyes were looking for telltale signs, for anything that would give him a hint of what she really was feeling. "So do I. Will it be any less white if we express what we feel for each other with our bodies?"

Her gaze shot up, her face flaming with bad temper. "That's all you feel for me, though. You said so. Wanting. You want me. I'm something you'd like to use…!"

He let her go abruptly, literally pushing her away from him. "My God, I can't get through to you, can I?" he asked bitterly.

She wrapped her arms across her breasts. "I wouldn't put it like that," she replied. "You wanted me four years ago, but you married Miriam. You loved her, not me."

"Four years ago, Miriam told me she was pregnant," he said, his face hardening at the memory. "By the time I realized she wasn't, we were married."

Her face tightened. She knew what he was saying. He and Miriam had anticipated their wedding vows. Probably by the time he'd made love to her at the swimming hole, he'd already been intimate with Miriam. She felt sick.

She started past him, but he caught her arms and held her. "No!" he said roughly. "It wasn't like that! It was you from the very beginning. Miriam was the substitute, Arabella, not you." He pulled her back against him, his teeth grinding together in anguish. "I knew that afternoon that if I didn't do something, I'd have you in spite of all my noble intentions. Miriam was handy and willing." He bent his head over hers. "I used her, and she knew it, and hated me for it. I cheated all three of us. She came to me and told me she thought she was pregnant, so I married her. You had your career and I didn't think you were old enough to cope with marriage, so I let you go. My God, don't you think I paid for that decision? I paid for it for four long years. I'm still paying!"

Time slowed to a standstill as what he was saying penetrated her mind. "You made love to Miriam because you wanted me?" she asked wanly. That was just what Miriam had said. That it had been a physical obsession on his part.

"Yes," he said with a heavy sigh. His fingers smoothed over the fabric of her sweater, caressing her shoulders. "And couldn't have you." His mouth pressed her hair away from her neck and sought it, warm and hard and fiercely passionate. "I wouldn't have been able to stop, Arabella," he whispered huskily. "Once I had you, I couldn't have stopped." His mouth opened, warm and moist against the tender flesh, arousing and slow. "You'd never have been able to leave, don't you see, baby? You'd have been mine. Totally mine."

Her eyes closed as the arousing movement of his lips made her knees go weak. He was seducing her with words. She shouldn't let him do this to her. She was weak.

He edged her into the deserted barn, against the inside

of the closed door, so that the weight of his lean body pinned her there from breast to thighs. He shuddered with his need.

"I'm going to make you marry me," he said into her mouth. "If it takes seduction, that's all right, too. I'll get you to the altar anyway I have to."

"Blackmailer," she protested shakenly.

"Kiss me back." He moved against her and felt her begin to tremble. Her mouth lifted and he took it with slow, aching movements that made her moan under the crush of the kiss, that made her give it back in a feverish surge of passion.

A long time later, he dragged her arms from around his neck and stepped away from her, a reddish burn along his cheeks, a tremor in the lean, sure hands that held her wrists.

"You can have a month," he said with savage hunger just barely held in check. "If the ring isn't on your finger by then, look out. I won't wait a night longer."

He turned and left her there, still shaking, with her back to the wall.

Exactly one month later, she spoke her vows in the small Jacobsville Methodist church with her father there to give her away and half of Jacobsville in attendance. Ethan hadn't touched her since that day in the barn, but his eyes threatened her every time he looked at her. He might not love her, but his passion for her was as alive and hot as the weather.

Miriam had long since gone back to the Caribbean with Jared, and she'd sent them a wedding invitation. She'd beaten Ethan to the altar by two weeks, but Ethan hadn't seemed to mind. He'd been busy, and away a good bit recently on ranch business. Coreen remarked dryly that it was probably just as well, because his moods were making everyone nervous.

Only Arabella understood exactly what those moods were about, and tonight she was going to have to cope with the cause of them. He'd reserved a hotel room for them at a resort on the Gulf of Mexico, and she was more nervous than she'd ever been in her life. All the walls were going to come down and she'd be alone with Ethan and his fierce desire for her. She didn't know how she was going to survive a possession that was purely physical.

"You made a beautiful bride," Coreen said, kissing her just before she went upstairs to change. She wiped away tears. "I just know you and Ethan are going to make it this time."

"I hope so," Arabella confessed, radiant despite her fears as she paused to kiss Mary and Matt and to thank Shelby.

"It was my pleasure," Shelby assured her, and tightened her grip on her tall husband's hand. Justin Ballenger was altogether too much man for the average woman, but Shelby had moved in under his heart, and he looked as if he didn't mind one bit. He smiled down at her, his lean face briefly radiant as his dark eyes swept over her with possession and pride.

"I won't forget all you've done for me," Arabella murmured, a little shy of Justin. She leaned forward and kissed Shelby's cheek. "Thank you."

"I hope you'll be very happy," Shelby said gently.

"You get out of marriage what you put into it," Justin added and smiled at her. "Give a little and take a little. You'll do fine."

"Thanks," Arabella replied.

He and Shelby moved off, hand in hand, and Arabella watched them with pure envy.

Ethan caught her hand, pulling her around. He searched her eyes with a light in his that puzzled her. It was the first time he'd come near her since he'd said, "I do," and he hadn't kissed her at the altar, to everyone's surprise and puzzlement.

"The luggage is in the car. Let's go," he said quietly, his eyes narrowing as they smoothed over her body. "I want you to myself."

"But…aren't we going to change?" she faltered.

"No." He framed her face in his lean hands and pulled it up to the descent of his. "I want to take that dress off you myself," he whispered, and his lips touched hers in a promise of a kiss that made her knees go weak. "Come along, Mrs. Hardeman."

He made the name sound new and sweet. She took his hand and let him lead her out, coping somehow with the shock and amusement of all the people who'd gathered around them here. The reception was supposed to be held in the fellowship hall, but Ethan had apparently decided that they were going to forego the traditional celebration. He grinned, whispered something to his delighted mother, and they left in a hail of rice and confetti and good wishes.

They drove to Galveston in his mother's Mercedes-Benz, since his own car had been left as a decoy for well-wishers with their soap and tin cans. His mother's car was untouched, and he grinned at Arabella's expression when she saw it.

"We're too old for all that," he chided as he put her in the car. "Tin cans and soaped windows—my God."

She made a face at him. "Some of us sure grow up too fast," she muttered.

"Not quite fast enough, in your case." He started the car and took off around the back of the church, glancing with amusement at the rear-view mirror where he could see a few friends were just staring after them with astonished faces. "I could very happily have married you at the age of sixteen, but I had a guilty conscience about robbing the cradle."

She was faintly shocked at the admission, not sure if she should even take the remark seriously. But he wasn't smiling.

"Don't believe me?" he asked with a quick glance. "Wait until we get to Galveston. You've got a lot of surprises coming."

"Have I?" She wondered what they were. She had a feeling the biggest one was going to be the wedding night she'd secretly dreaded. Love on one side wasn't going to be enough to get her through that, and she knew it.

He kept music playing until they reached the lovely brick hotel on the beach and checked in. Their room overlooked the beach and Galveston Bay, and it was a remote spot, for all its closeness to town. Sea gulls dipped down on the beach and she watched them wistfully.

"Change into some jeans and a top and we'll walk down the beach," he suggested, sensing her discomfort. "It's a bit cool today for swimming."

"Okay." She hesitated, wondering if he was going to expect her to undress in front of him.

"You can have the bathroom. I'll change in here," he said easily.

She gave him a grateful smile and got her things out of her suitcase. By the time she'd changed into her jeans and a gray pullover shirt, he was wearing jeans and a blue-and-white striped shirt.

"Let's go." He didn't give her time to be self-conscious about sharing the big room with its two double beds. He led her out onto the beach and they spent the afternoon looking for shells and talking. Later they had a seafood supper in a restaurant located in an old lighthouse, and sat on the big deck after dark and watched the ships pass.

By the time they went back into their room, Arabella was relaxed and so much in love that she didn't even protest when Ethan took her in his arms in the doorway and began to kiss her with fervent hunger.

He didn't turn on the light. He closed and locked the door in the dark and picked Arabella up, carrying her to the first of the two beds.

She was lost in his hard, deep kisses, in the caressing movements of his lean hands as he undressed her with slow delight, discovering her body with his lips first, then his hands. She stretched like a cat while he undressed and when she felt the first touch of his naked skin against her own, she gasped with shocked pleasure.

His mouth covered hers then, gentling her. As the minutes began to move faster, as the heat began to burn inside her, as the kisses grew endless and his hands made her shiver and cry out, she forgot her fear and gave him what he wanted. When he moved over her, she welcomed the hard thrust of his body with trusting abandon.

He pushed down and she clung to him. There was a

flash of pain, and then it was feverish movement and growing pleasure that finally exploded into an ecstasy that bordered on pain in its sweeping fulfillment.

"No," he groaned when she made a hesitant movement, aeons later. His hands swept her back, hard against him, and he shuddered as he held her there, against his sweat-dampened body. "Stay here."

"Are you all right?" she whispered into his throat.

"Now, I am," he replied. His lips brushed tenderly over her face. "You love me. We couldn't have made love like this out of desire alone," he whispered huskily. "Not with this kind of tenderness."

She closed her eyes. So he knew. It wasn't surprising. That had probably been her biggest fear, that when he made love to her, he was going to realize how much she cared.

Her fingers moved gently in his thick, damp hair. "Yes," she confessed then. "I love you. I always have. I don't think they've invented a cure for it."

"God forbid that they ever should," he whispered back. He cradled her intimately in the curve of his legs with a long sigh. His hand smoothed over her waist, her breast, with slow possession and he laughed. "You're mine," he said with gruff amusement. "I'm never going to let you go now. You're going to live with me and bear my children and we're going to be everything to each other for the rest of our lives."

"Even though you only want me?" she asked sadly.

"I want you, yes," he replied. His hands smoothed her back against him, so that her body could feel the urgent press of his. "I want you to the point of madness and beyond. If it were only desire that I felt, any woman's body would do. But that isn't the case." He held her hips to his. "Not only was there no Miriam, there was no other woman for four years. Is that enough proof of love?"

Her breath caught. She turned in his grasp, her eyes trying to see his through the moonlit darkness. "You love me?"

"My God, with all my heart," he said huskily. "You little blind fool, didn't you know? My mother did. Mary and Matt did. Everyone knew what I felt, including Miriam, so why didn't you?"

She laughed, on fire with the first daring certainty of shared love, belonging. "Because I was a blind little fool! Oh, Ethan, I love you, I love you, I love...!"

That was as far as she got. He rolled her into him and his hands grew quickly urgent, like the hard mouth that had cut off her hasty admission. He moved against her and she moved to accommodate him, and for a long time, they said nothing while their bodies spoke in a new and intimate language of love.

"God knows how I'll share you with the stage," he groaned much later when they were propped up together sharing a soft drink he'd retrieved from the refrigerator in the room. "But I'll manage."

"Oh. That." She grimaced and laid her face against his warm, bare shoulder. "Well, I sort of lied."

"What?"

"I sort of lied," she repeated. "I will be able to use my hand again, and play again, but not like I did before." She sighed, nuzzling her cheek against him with a loving sigh. "I can teach, but I can't perform. And before you say it, I'm not sorry. I'd rather have you than be as great as Van Cliburn."

He couldn't speak. If he needed proof of her love,

that gave it to him. He bent and kissed her eyes with breathless tenderness. "Truly, Arabella?" he asked softly.

"Truly, Ethan." She nibbled at his lips and simultaneously set the ice-cold bottom of the soft drink on his warm, flat belly.

His voice exploded in the darkness and he jumped. Arabella laughed with endless delight, anticipating a delicious reprisal.

"Why, you little..." he began, and she could see the smile, hear the loving threat, see the quick movement in her direction.

She put the drink on the bedside table and reached out to him, drawing him to her, accepting her fate with arms that would accept everything life had to offer for the rest of her life. Ethan in her arms. Heaven.

* * * * *

THE
Essential
COLLECTION

by Diana Palmer

YES! Please send me *The Essential Collection* by Diana Palmer. This collection will begin with 3 FREE BOOKS and 2 FREE GIFTS in my very first shipment—and more valuable free gifts will follow! My books will arrive in 8 monthly shipments until I have the entire 51-book *Essential Collection* by Diana Palmer. I will receive 2 free books in each shipment and I will pay just $4.49 U.S./$5.39 CDN for each of the other 4 books in each shipment, plus $2.99 for shipping and handling.* If I decide to keep the entire collection, I'll only have paid for 32 books because 19 books are free. I understand that accepting the 3 free books and gifts places me under no obligation to buy anything. I can always return a shipment and cancel at any time. My free books and gifts are mine to keep no matter what I decide.

279 HDK 9860   479 HDK 9860

Name	(PLEASE PRINT)
Address	Apt. #
City State/Prov.	Zip/Postal Code

Signature (if under 18, a parent or guardian must sign)

Mail to the **Reader Service:**
IN U.S.A.: P.O. Box 1867, Buffalo, NY 14240-1867
IN CANADA: P.O. Box 609, Fort Erie, Ontario L2A 5X3

* Terms and prices subject to change without notice. Prices do not include applicable taxes. Sales tax applicable in N.Y. Canadian residents will be charged applicable taxes. This offer is limited to one order per household. All orders subject to credit approval. Credit or debit balances in a customer's account(s) may be offset by any other outstanding balance owed by or to the customer. Please allow 4–6 weeks for delivery. Offer available while quantities last. Offer not available to Quebec residents.

Your Privacy—The Reader Service is committed to protecting your privacy. Our Privacy Policy is available online at www.ReaderService.com or upon request from the Reader Service.

We make a portion of our mailing list available to reputable third parties that offer products we believe may interest you. If you prefer that we not exchange your name with third parties, or if you wish to clarify or modify your communication preferences, please visit us at www.ReaderService.com/consumerschoice or write to us at Reader Service Preference Service, P.O. Box 9062, Buffalo, NY 14269. Include your complete name and address.